Sammy planted a sloppy kiss on Cooper's cheek. Then he trotted away.

Cooper sat down on a nearby bench and took out his phone. While he scrolled through for the right number, Bree dropped into a chair shaped like an overturned tortoiseshell, and he could feel those penetrating eyes on him.

Without looking up, he asked, "What?"

"That's the sweetest thing I've ever seen in my life." He glanced over to find her beaming at him. "You, Mayor Landry, are a very nice man."

"You sound surprised."

"I am."

He'd gotten accustomed to her firm way of speaking, so the softness in her tone caught him off guard. She was a full arm's length away, but the warmth in her eyes reached the vulnerable part of him that had shut down. He couldn't fathom how Bree had done that so quickly, but he couldn't deny she'd found her way there.

This was dangerous territory for him.

Books by Mia Ross

Love Inspired

  Hometown Family
  Circle of Family
  A Gift of Family
  A Place for Family
*Rocky Coast Romance

*Holiday Harbor

MIA ROSS

loves great stories. She enjoys reading about fascinating people, long-ago times and exotic places. But only for a little while, because her reality is pretty sweet. Married to her college sweetheart, she's the proud mom of two amazing kids, whose schedules keep her hopping. Busy as she is, she can't imagine trading her life for anyone else's—and she has a pretty good imagination. You can visit her online at www.miaross.com.

Rocky Coast Romance
Mia Ross

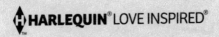

HARLEQUIN® LOVE INSPIRED®

Recycling programs for this product may not exist in your area.

™ LOVE INSPIRED BOOKS

ISBN-13: 978-0-373-87832-1

ROCKY COAST ROMANCE

Copyright © 2013 by Andrea Chermak

www.LoveInspiredBooks.com

Printed in U.S.A.

What is seen is temporary,
but what is unseen is eternal.
—*2 Corinthians* 4:18

For Misty

Acknowledgments

To the very talented folks who help me make my books everything they can be: Elaine Spencer, Melissa Endlich, Rachel Burkot and the dedicated staff at Love Inspired Books.

More thanks to the gang at Seekerville (www.seekerville.net). Whether I'm looking for advice or just some cheerleaders, you never let me down.

My wonderful—and very patient— friends and family surround me with support and encouragement every single day. Without you, this book would still just be an idea floating around in my head.

Chapter One

~

"Comin' in to Hahliday Hahbah!"

The driver's announcement cut through her sound-canceling headphones, and Bree Farrell glanced up from the movie playing on her tablet computer. Outside the grimy window she saw a whole lot of nothing. Then the bus lumbered over a hill, and on the other side was a town.

Surrounded by endless miles of ocean, Holiday Harbor looked like it was barely clinging to the rugged Maine coastline. Off in the distance a rotating beacon drew her eye to a lighthouse that looked as if it had sprouted from the rocky cliff it was perched on.

All very nice poetic descriptions, she thought, opening her notes file to capture her observations before they vanished. A born and bred city girl, she wasn't crazy about this edge-of-the-world assignment her prospective editor had given her. But a long string of missteps and bad choices had drained her savings account and left her with a less than stellar reputation.

And no options. If she couldn't wrangle a permanent byline at *Kaleidoscope,* she'd have to dust off her waitressing skills and move back in with her mom. Determined to avoid such drastic measures, she knew she had to make this article shine.

When the bus pulled into the center of town, she stayed in her seat, waiting for the other passengers to collect small bags from the overhead bins. While they gathered their things, she took the opportunity to jot down descriptions of them. Since it was just after noon on a Thursday, she assumed they were all here for the Fourth of July weekend. There were three Italian suit types, a few in jeans and sneakers and a dreamy young couple wearing bride and groom T-shirts.

Glancing out the window again, she decided that while it wouldn't be her first choice for a honeymoon destination, Holiday Harbor did have a certain quiet charm about it. Far from the crowded streets of Richmond, Virginia, she'd probably feel like the clichéd fish out of water. A jolt of nerves shot up her back, and she took a deep breath to regain her composure.

She'd made some careless mistakes in her past, but she was a pro. This was her chance to prove it to everyone who'd written her off as flaky and difficult to work with.

And to herself.

Stepping onto the cracked sidewalk, she caught the unmistakable scent of salt water and fish, laced with the pungent diesel that powered the small fleet of fishing boats chugging to and from a busy set of docks. Another interesting tidbit, and she scribbled it down with her stylus.

"You must be Bree Farrell."

The mellow voice startled her, and she clutched her tablet close to her chest. Her parents had stopped fighting long enough to buy it for her as a birthday gift, and nobody was taking her prized possession from her without a serious fight. In her next breath she realized how stupid her reaction was. Even in the worst places she'd visited, thieves didn't stroll over and address you by name.

Looking up, she found herself staring at the collar of a dark blue polo shirt. When her eyes moved up a little farther, she got the surprise of her life.

Someone had planted a movie star in her path. With eyes the color of a clear sky and an easygoing smile, the stranger who'd come to greet her would weaken the knees of any female over ten and still breathing. He had broad shoulders and a lean, athletic physique to die for. Dressed in nicely pressed chinos and deck shoes, he looked like he was headed out for a sail.

When she realized he was waiting for her to respond, she jerked herself back to the moment. "Must I?"

Chuckling, he offered a hand. "Cooper Landry. Welcome to Holiday Harbor."

"Landry." They'd never met, she was certain of that. But the name rang a bell, and she asked, "Are you related to Mayor George Landry?"

His eyes darkened, and his welcoming smile faltered before righting itself. "Actually, I'm the mayor now."

Bree was usually pretty good at gauging someone's age, but with his windblown good looks, this guy could be anywhere from twenty-five to forty. While she mulled that over, she noted that the logo on his shirt wasn't a name brand but a sketch of a sailboat, with the words *Holiday Harbor* floating like waves beneath it. Promoting the village on that solid chest of his, she thought with a grin. Nice touch.

"Aren't you a little young to be a mayor?"

"I'm thirty, but thanks for the compliment."

Only a couple of years older than her, she thought with a frown. "Isn't that a lot of responsibility for someone your age?"

"I guess it is." He shrugged as if it hadn't occurred to him until she brought it up. "Granddad passed away a few months ago, and the town asked me to complete the rest of his term."

"I'm so sorry," she stammered. Again she'd waded into deep water before thinking things through. "My research must be a little out of date."

"Not your fault, but thanks."

After a moment he added another, more personal smile. It was the kind of gesture that lit up his eyes and made her feel like he was honestly glad to see her. Lately she hadn't gotten that kind of reaction from too many people, and it made her feel slightly more at ease.

Trying to make conversation, she said, "I'm not used to being met by the mayor when I'm on assignment somewhere. That was nice of you."

"It only seemed right. I'm the one who asked *Kaleidoscope* to send someone to do a story here."

His comment piqued her curiosity. "Really? The magazine is pretty new, and online besides. What made you think of it?"

"Your editor, Nick McHenry, grew up here, and we go way back. He thought we'd make a great addition to the Americana series he's running this summer." The driver set Bree's two bags in front of her, and her host handed him five dollars. "Thanks, Ed. Are you and your wife gonna make it up here for the Fourth?"

The older man's face broke into a delighted grin. "We

wouldn't miss it. We've got the grandkids right now, and they can't wait."

"If you've got time, stop by my place for some barbecue. After you eat, you can get ringside seats for the fireworks. Red Granger's in charge of them again, and he promised they'd be even better than last year's."

Respect flooded Ed's expression, and Bree figured he didn't often get invitations to visit a town leader at his home. "We'll do that. Thanks."

"Great! We'll see you then."

They shook hands to seal the deal, and Ed closed the cargo doors before climbing aboard.

As the bus chugged away, Cooper eyed Bree's scant luggage in disbelief. "Is this it?"

"Yeah." She slung her beat-up messenger bag across her chest. "Reporters travel light." She didn't add that the pilot's case and small duffel held the extent of her wardrobe.

"We keep traffic out of the center of town to leave room to walk for pedestrians, so I had to park down the street." Without asking, he shouldered her duffel and lifted her suitcase. "I apologize for the hike."

Bree almost told him she could manage her own bags, but something stopped her. It might come across as rude, and she didn't want to insult him by refusing his hospitality. Her last termination notice flashed into her mind like a recurring nightmare.

Talented but headstrong. Impossible to work with.

Not this time, she vowed. This time she'd choke down her instincts and be a team player. Even if it killed her.

"No problem," she said lightly. "It'll give me a feel for the town."

They started walking, and he asked, "Have you eaten, Miss Farrell?"

Knowing this could be her last chance at her dream career, she'd only managed to choke down half a ham and cheese sandwich while waiting for the bus. Unwilling to admit how nervous she was about this assignment, she replied, "I had lunch at the airport in Rockland while I was waiting for the bus, so I'm fine. And it's Bree."

"Then I'm Cooper. I'm sort of named after the founder of this place. He was from a long line of barrel makers."

"Interesting." That sounded lame, so she added what she hoped was a pleasant smile and started checking out her surroundings.

Main Street was lined with old buildings, some made of brick, others of the weathered clapboards Maine was famous for. The shops' front doors and display windows were shaded by identical light blue awnings, and flowers of every color overflowed from window boxes and hanging pots. In the center of town was a gazebo surrounded by a small park where several kids were kicking a soccer ball around.

Everywhere she looked she saw American flags and bunting, obviously set out for Monday's Fourth of July festivities. She could have thrown a rock the length of the business district, but it did occupy both sides of the street. It included a diner, a small café and something she'd assumed had all but gone extinct.

"A real bookstore," she commented. "I can't remember the last time I saw one of those."

"They carry lots of things, even some antique books. My mother owns it, and she has a huge collection. If you want, I can set up a tour for you."

"That would be awesome," she blurted, then realized she sounded like a teenager with a crush. Acting unprofessionally had caused her more trouble than even her vivid imagination could have invented. Getting a firmer grip on her dignity, she amended, "If I have time."

Across the street was a store called There's No Place Like Gnome, which apparently sold nothing but garden statues so ugly they were cute. It was totally unexpected, and Bree made a quick note of it. Unique features like that would be great for her story. An award-winning reporter himself, Nick McHenry was notoriously tough to impress, and she was desperate to earn his confidence. To do that, she'd have to knock this article out of the park.

"I see six vacant storefronts." She paused in the middle of the sidewalk for a better look. Their display windows were clean but dark, and while the For Rent signs were subtly posted in lower corners, you couldn't miss them. "Is the economy especially bad here?"

"Unfortunately, yes. Fish and seafood stocks are declining, taking the towns that rely on that industry right along with them. That's why you're here. We need to bring in more tourists, to help fill the gap."

It sounded like a solid plan, but she knew better than anyone that things didn't always work out the way you wanted them to. "And if they don't come?"

Worry clouded his expression, and he grimaced. "There's another option, but I don't like to think about it."

"But you have," she pressed. "I can tell."

"We all have," he admitted with a sigh. "There's a developer who wants to come in and build a golf community outside of town. We just can't agree whether to say yes or no."

This would be news to Nick, she was certain of it. If she did some digging and asked the right questions around town, maybe she could parlay the development issue into another article. Or even a series of them. Having scraped her savings account down to the bone, the influx of cash would be a refreshing change.

For now she put aside her own interests and went the sympathetic route. It wasn't hard, since to even mention it to a stranger, the potential construction project must be weighing heavily on his mind. "That must make mayoring kind of hard, especially since you didn't run for the office."

Cooper eyed her with something she hadn't seen much of the past year: respect. "Off the record?"

Bree held up her hands to show him she wasn't recording or taking notes of any kind. "Of course."

"You're very perceptive, and you're right. I didn't want the job, and it's turning out to be a lot tougher than I thought it'd be. But I love this place, and I'm doing my best to keep things on track until we elect someone else in the fall. My personal situation has nothing to do with why you're here, so let's just focus on the town. Okay?"

He was so upbeat, even in the face of what must be a huge problem, she couldn't help smiling. Some people honestly believed that positive thinking led to positive outcomes, and she wasn't going to be the one to burst this handsome optimist's bubble. "Okay."

His assessment couldn't have been more wrong, but she opted to keep that opinion to herself. The state of Holiday Harbor's town government had everything to do with its problems—and the potential solutions to them. If she'd learned anything during her varied assignments, it was that there were several facets to every story. Her job was to uncover as many of them as possible and give her readers all the angles.

They continued walking, and beyond the modest business district, Victorian-style homes rose up behind white picket fences. Their porch roofs were accented in crisp white gingerbread, their yards filled with neatly trimmed hedges and flower gardens. It was like stepping into a living, breathing Norman Rockwell painting. Even though she was seeing it for herself, Bree couldn't quite believe a place like this still existed.

In front of one hung a brass sign that read Landry House—1820. During her research, she'd learned that was the year Maine had attained statehood, which meant the Landrys had been here a very long time. The yellow house had a cheerful presence, with tall windows and a wing on either side to balance out the porch running along the front. Well-tended flower beds led to two rows of petunias that bordered the wide walkway leading to the porch.

Large and inviting, it was nothing like the apartments Bree had grown up in. Always seeking new experiences, her restless parents had moved from one city to the next, so she'd never been in one place more than a year. Being so deeply rooted didn't appeal to her, but obviously it worked for Cooper's family.

"On the record now?" she asked.

There was that grin again. This time she caught a faint dimple in one cheek that gave him a little boy look she hadn't noticed before. "Sure."

"Tell me about Holiday Harbor." She discreetly hit the record button on her phone. The video would be of the inside of her pocket, but the sound should be good enough for her to take notes from later.

"Back in 1816, my ancestor William Landry—"

He paused for a proud grin, and she smiled. "The cooper."

"That's the one. Anyway, he started up the coast with four wagons and a hand-drawn map from a blacksmith in Concord, Massachusetts. He claimed there was untouched land up here, sitting right on the ocean, where a man could farm or fish, or both. His brother and new wife joined them, along with a few other families. On Christmas Day, they ended up here."

"Literally the end of the road."

Bree wondered how those long-ago travelers had felt when they saw this place for the first time. Relieved that their long journey was over? Or regretting that they'd left civilization so far behind?

"Back then it was nothing but wilderness, but he liked it right away. So he got down off his wagon, looked around and said to his wife, 'This is it, Addie. We'll call it Holiday Harbor, in honor of our Lord's birth.' My family's been here ever since."

This was the kind of story people adored, and while Bree recognized she'd have to confirm every last detail except the name of the town, the yarn had a nice ring to it. In keeping with the village's old-fashioned appearance, she'd call the article "Mayberry on the Sea." "Nick told me you celebrate some unusual holidays up here."

"Yeah, we do. Most months there's a traditional holiday. When there's not, we find something and make our own festival out of it."

"So this month it's the Fourth of July. What's in August?"

"The seventh is always National Lighthouse Day. We'll have a picnic in the square, bring in kiddie rides, carnival games, stuff like that. It'll also be the fourth round of the Holiday Harbor Costume Regatta, which runs from May to September every year."

Bree had heard lots of odd things, but this was a new one for her. "You mean people sail their boats dressed in costumes?"

"People, pets, whatever. Some folks even dress up their boats."

That sounded intriguing, and slightly insane. In other words, ideal for her purposes. "Are you competing in the race on the Fourth of July?"

"Of course," he said, as if that should have been obvious. "My sailboat *Stargazer* won the cup last year."

It was so cute, the way he gave his boat all the credit. Most guys she knew would brag about their sailing prowess, but not this one. She found his humility a refreshing change.

They seemed to have reached the end of the town history, so she switched tracks. "Sailing attire aside, you don't strike me as a small-town guy. What's your story, Mr. Mayor?"

"Yale Law School, fast track to partner at a big firm in New York City. A hundred hours a week, no life. One day I realized I hated what I was doing and decided to come home. I went into business with my grandfather, and took over the law firm when he passed away."

From his expression, she suspected there was more to the story than he'd confided, but she decided it was best to let him off the hook for now. Early in her career she'd learned that when she pushed for too much too fast, people tended to stop talking. "What kind of law do you practice?"

"All kinds. Real estate, wills, trusts, the occasional court case."

The last item snagged her attention. "Any juicy trials recently?"

"Not unless you count a neighborly dispute over a horse."

He was totally deadpan, and she didn't realize he was pulling her leg until she caught the mischievous gleam in his eyes. It took her a few seconds, then it clicked. "*Neigh*-bor. I get it."

"Get what?"

The gleam was still there, and she smiled. "You're really good at that. You must've been awesome in front of a judge."

Bree's compliment tweaked a sensitive nerve, taking Cooper back to when he still believed his litigating success was all his own doing. Finding out otherwise had all but destroyed him. To mask his discomfort, he summoned the professional smile that had served him well in courtrooms and boardrooms alike. Pleasant but unreadable, during law school he'd practiced it in front of a mirror until he was satisfied he'd produced just the right effect. It had gotten him through a lot of difficult meetings during his career.

At least this encounter came with a fantastic view. Even without the last name he'd have known the pretty reporter had some Irish in her. The sun picked up strands of red in her curly brown ponytail, while highlighting a generous dusting of freckles across her cheeks. The effect was pixieish, completely at odds with the intelligence crackling in her dark eyes.

During his time in New York, Cooper had dated more than his share of models and actresses, the kind of women most people would consider perfection. But Bree Farrell, with her fair skin and forthright manner, was the most captivating woman he'd met in a long time.

Because that train of thought would only lead him into trouble, he shoved it aside and focused on more practical things. "It's not a quick trip up here from Virginia. You must be ready for a nap."

"That would be great," she agreed with a sigh. "My plane left Richmond early this morning, and it's been kind of a weird day."

"How do you mean?"

As if on cue, David Birdsall, dressed in the height of nineteenth-century fashion, pedaled down the street on his tall antique bicycle. Bree gave Cooper a little smile, arching a single eyebrow that clearly said she had all the ammunition she needed to portray Holiday Harbor as a quaint seaside lunatic asylum.

Cooper grinned back. "That's different. You can't just jump on one of those things and make it work, you know. It takes practice."

"Why is he riding it in the first place?"

"Monday's our Independence Day celebration. He always hauls it out for that."

"And the outfit?"

To an outsider it must look ridiculous, and Cooper couldn't help chuckling. "That's just a bonus."

"Interesting."

She'd said that before, and he got the distinct impression she was going out of her way not to aggravate him.

Unfortunately her efforts were having the opposite effect, and he cautioned himself to be patient. Cynical and way too smart for her own good, he had the feeling she was going to batter his sleepy little town like a nor'easter.

"There are two weddings in town this weekend, and the inn on Main Street is full up," he explained. "The Harbor Mansion's being refurbished and won't be ready for a couple more weeks."

She frowned. "So am I camping out somewhere?"

"No need for that. There's a room at the lighthouse for you. I called in some favors, and you can stay out there for free as long as you're here. It's small, but the view's amazing."

"I saw it on my way in," she said hesitantly, "and it's kind of far away. I was hoping to spend most of my time here in town, talking to people."

"Don't worry," he assured her. "I borrowed my mom's spare car for you and left it at the lighthouse. Nothing fancy, but it runs well and should get you where you need to go."

"Thanks. I'm sure that'll be fine."

Cooper detected a slight strain in her tone. Raised by his single mother, he was no stranger to feminine-speak. He was well aware that when a woman said things were "fine," it was time to start worrying. Since there was nothing he could do about it, he chose to ignore her comment and forge ahead.

He paused beside a burgundy four-by-four with no top or doors, and she turned to him with a shocked look. "This is yours?"

"Uh-huh."

"Where's the rest of it?"

Tossing her bags into the back, he laughed. "It's so nice today, I decided to go open-air. You've never ridden in one stripped down like this?"

"I've never ridden in one of these, period. A lawyer who drives a four-by-four," she muttered, climbing into the passenger seat. "Now I've seen everything."

"You haven't been here that long." Taking his aviator sunglasses from their clip on the visor, he put them on and started the engine. "You never know what other surprises we've got."

In response she tilted her cute little nose in the air, but he'd witnessed enough courtroom drama to suspect her confident demeanor was mostly an act.

As he pulled away from the curb, he said, "I think you'll find the folks around here aren't like other people you've met. They're proud of being unique."

"Then we should get along well. I'm not like other people I've met, either."

He slanted her a quick glance. "Are you trying to be a pain, or are you just naturally prickly?"

"Yes."

Pointedly ignoring him, she slipped on a pair of big, Hollywood-style sunglasses. Cooper knew almost nothing about his passenger, but Nick had warned him that her latest bungle had turned Bree into a virtual leper. His old buddy was the only editor—print or online—with the guts to hire her. During their brief conversation, Cooper had noticed plenty of attitude, not to mention a good-sized chip on her shoulder.

Still, he couldn't imagine what she might have done to warrant the blackballing she'd received. In his very first Sunday school class, he'd learned that everyone deserved to be forgiven if they truly regretted what they'd done. As he got older, his mother had told him more than once that the people who seemed to want it the least needed it the most.

It was possible that the sarcastic young woman beside him was one of those people.

From the corner of his eye he saw Bree slide her tablet from her messenger bag. When she tried to wake the screen, she groaned. "You've *got* to be kidding me."

"That won't work out here, but there's internet at the lighthouse, to keep track of the satellite weather reports. You should be able to connect to that."

She eyed the distant beacon with no enthusiasm at all. "It's kind of isolated out there. Us city girls are used to working where there's things going on. There must be a café in town with an open connection."

"Nope."

Clearly horrified by the lack of technology in Holiday Harbor, she nudged her glasses down and scowled at him in the rearview mirror. "If you want people to come visit this place, you've got to bring it into the twenty-first century."

"Don't folks go on vacation to get away from all that?" Focused on the two-lane road that wound its way toward the ocean, he motioned to her tablet. "I mean, most days when I get home, I'm happy to turn it all off and go for a sail."

"That's nice for you, but for the rest of us, modern technology makes the world go 'round."

Prickly *and* hard to please, he thought with a mental groan. Just what he needed. But she was his guest, and her impression of Holiday Harbor would undoubtedly affect the way she depicted the town to her readers. Keeping her happy was in everyone's best interest. "I've got Wi-Fi at my office. You're welcome to use it instead."

"I just might take you up on that."

"Anytime. It's on Main Street, in the cream-colored building next to the gnome store."

That got him a short, sarcastic laugh. "Of course it is."

He'd finally had enough. But when he shot her a glare, it made no impression at all because she was staring in the other direction. He came dangerously close to giving her a piece of his mind, but decided to give her a break. She'd called herself a city girl, and the quaint fishing village must feel as alien to her as the face of the moon. He'd just have to show her how beautiful his hometown was.

For her article, of course. Intriguing as she might be under all that attitude, her personal opinion couldn't possibly matter less to him.

"Here it is," he announced as they crested the last rise and descended toward the water's edge. "Last Chance Lighthouse."

Chapter Two

Cooper stopped at the end of a dirt lane, putting the car in Park as Bree took out her camera and stood up for an unobstructed view. When she let out a dreamy sigh, he leaned back in his seat and smiled. Mission accomplished.

"This is amazing," she breathed.

A driveway crisscrossed with ruts led out to the rocky point topped by the lighthouse. The breeze coming off the water came and went, whipping her ponytail around one second and dying off the next. Waves crashed against the outcropping of unforgiving rocks, which had taken down several ships before the warning beacon was finally built.

Seagulls circled overhead, calling out to each other as they glided through the air. Cooper watched Bree expertly single out one that appeared to be zooming in on something under the surf. Rapidly snapping frame after frame, she followed the bird as it dropped down and came out with a fish.

"It's pretty," she said, as if the description had just

occurred to her. "In a salty-around-the-edges kind of way, y'know?"

"Yeah, I think so, too."

"You almost expect to see the ghost of some old sea captain standing on the balcony, staring out to sea, looking for the ship he lost years ago."

The fanciful image surprised him, mostly because with just a few words, she'd painted a picture in his mind he wasn't likely to forget anytime soon. She had a real gift, he thought with a smile. He wondered if she knew how incredible she was. *It* was, he corrected himself quickly, relieved that he'd had the good sense not to be thinking out loud.

Craning her neck, she surveyed the area hopefully and then sighed. "You're kidding. There's nothing else out here."

He'd come to terms with her less-than-flattering perspective of his home, so this time Cooper chuckled as he put the car in Drive and turned onto the lane. "The keeper's widow, Mavis Freeman, runs a B and B for special guests. Very exclusive, like the finest hotels."

He flashed Bree a grin and was pleased to hear her laugh. He congratulated himself on prying some levity out of the very intense young woman who'd landed in his town.

"Mavis doesn't warm up to strangers right away," he warned as they left the car and climbed a few stone steps worn down by decades of wind-driven sand. There was no doorbell or knocker, so he pulled the rope on the brass ship's bell next to the bright red door. "Just be patient with her."

Bree seemed so taken with the place, he wasn't sure

she'd heard him. He was about to caution her again when the door swung inward on creaky iron hinges.

Mavis squinted up at him. "Who's there?"

"Where are your glasses?" Cooper demanded. "You know you're supposed to wear them all the time."

"Don't need 'em when I'm crocheting." Her cranky response told him she might have started out crocheting but had ended up napping. "You've got no business giving me orders, Cooper Landry. You're not the mayor on my island."

"Don't need to be," he assured her smoothly, ignoring the fact that technically the property was connected to the mainland. "You have everything under control out here."

"Got that right." Turning to Bree, Mavis gave her a puzzled once-over. "You must be that troublemaking reporter who's gonna be staying here."

"Yes, ma'am. It's a pleasure to meet you." Bree sounded almost humble, and he wondered where the politeness had come from all of a sudden. "Thanks so much for letting me camp out here. I promise not to get in the way of your very important work."

"Work?"

"The light." Bree waved toward the rotating signal. "Without the keepers here at Holiday Harbor, ships would break up on the rocks while they're coming into port. It's a huge responsibility."

Her earlier sarcasm was nowhere to be heard, and Cooper wondered if she'd taken his advice to heart or was deftly buttering up her hostess.

At any rate, Mavis stood a little taller and straightened the moth-eaten gray sweater she wore on even the warmest days. "Well, now, it's not often us keepers get that kind of respect. Folks generally take us for granted, figuring the light just runs on its own."

"Not me," Bree assured her warmly. "I've been all over the world, but I've never seen anything like this. I'd love to hear the history of this place, if you have time."

"Honey, I got nothing but time. You come right on in." She opened the door wide and let Bree through. Cooper she stopped with a gnarled hand on his chest. "You done good this time, Mr. Mayor. The judge'll be hearing from me, you can count on that."

"Granddad's been gone awhile now," he reminded her gently.

"I still talk to him up in Heaven," she retorted. "He hears me just fine."

She meant well, and despite his lingering sadness, Cooper managed to smile. "I'm sure he enjoys that. And I appreciate you putting in a good word for me."

"Don't you be going all soft on us, though." She pointed a crooked finger at him in warning. "This town's in trouble, and it needs strength, not coddling."

"Yes, ma'am. Speaking of strength, how's that new retaining wall holding up?"

"Like a champ. Those boys you sent did good work. They ate me out of gingerbread, though."

"That's because you make the best in the state."

"First place at the fair, seven years running," she boasted. "I've got some fresh if you think Miss Farrell would like some."

Cooper knew that was the height of hostess etiquette for the bristly woman, and he nodded. "I think she'd love it."

"Fine. Now be a good boy and help me find my glasses."

As they entered the dim front hallway, Cooper heard Bree's sharp gasp from up ahead. "Um, a little help here?"

She was flattened up against the wall, staring down at a black potbellied pig the size of a small beagle. He sat in front of her, tail scraping across the well-worn oak planks in a friendly greeting. Judging by the horrified look on her face, she didn't think much of her welcoming committee.

"Oh, that's just Reggie sayin' hello to you," Mavis told her. "He loves it when folks come by. Honestly," she added with a soft cackle, "he likes people better'n I do."

"Where on earth did you get a pig?" Bree asked, eyeing him cautiously.

"When my Henry died, God rest him." Closing her eyes, Mavis held a hand over her heart and looked down. After a respectful moment she lifted her head and continued. "I wasn't real fond of living by myself. Pastor Allen thought I'd do better if I had some company, so I went to the shelter over in Oakbridge, figuring to get a dog or a cat." Crouching down, she scratched Reggie behind his ears while he grunted in appreciation. "This little guy waddled over and sat down in front of me, and I knew he was the critter for me. He's housebroken and smart as a whip."

Clearly the skeptical journalist wasn't convinced. "Really?"

Mavis gave her a you'll-see grin. "Reggie?" The little porker rose to all fours, wagging his tail eagerly. "Snack time."

Delight flashed in his black eyes, and he trotted over to a set of open bookshelves. Grasping a plastic container in his teeth, he dragged it out but left it untouched, looking to Mavis for directions. She held up two fingers. "You can have two."

Grumbling his approval, he reached in with his snout and removed one piece of jerky, letting it fall on the floor before going after another. When he had them, he placed the container neatly back on its shelf and swooped up his reward before retreating into the parlor.

"Wow," Bree said, shaking her head. "That's really something."

Mavis's craggy face wrinkled into a proud smile. "That little guy's smarter'n most people I know. He's not much to look at, but then neither am I, and he don't seem to mind. You two go sit down. I'll put the teakettle on and slice up some gingerbread."

As she passed by him, Cooper stopped her with a hand on her shoulder. Giving her the glasses he'd found dangling from a hook on the coat stand, he said, "You might want these."

"No, but I'll take them all the same." Slipping them on, she looked him over from head to toe with a critical expression. "You need a woman, Cooper Landry. Eating too much of his own cooking makes a man skinny."

"You sound like Mom, right before she stuffs me full of pot roast."

"That's just plain nonsense," Mavis scoffed. "We're not a thing alike, and you know it."

He did, but no visit to the lighthouse was complete without a little good-natured sparring. Nose in the air, Mavis strolled through to the kitchen, and Bree glanced over at him, amusement sparkling in her eyes. She didn't say anything, but it didn't take much to figure out what was going through that quick mind of hers.

"I know she's a little eccentric," he murmured as

they walked into the sitting room, "but she's harmless, I promise."

Stretched out on the flagstone hearth, Reggie had obviously inhaled his first treat and was enthusiastically attacking the other.

Bree settled on the edge of an antique chair that had seen better days. She lifted one curious brow, the way she had when David Birdsall had pedaled down Main Street in his costume. "I have one question."

"Shoot."

"Is the whole town like this?"

"Well," Cooper stalled, searching for a way to skirt around the truth without lying. It was a survival skill he'd perfected during his courtroom career. But these days it just wasn't for him, so he shrugged. "I guess so."

Laughing, she added a note to her tablet. "Amazing."

Cooper wasn't quite sure what she meant by that, or if the comment was intended to be an insult or a compliment.

Maybe bringing in a stranger to write about Holiday Harbor wasn't such a good idea after all.

Bree was about as far from a tea and cookies kind of person as you could get, but Mavis's snack was a whole lot tastier than the dry half sandwich she'd choked down at the airport earlier. While they munched and chatted, she made a mental picture of her surroundings, from the rugged landscape framed in the bay window to the parlor itself.

Everything from the oval carpet to the carved mahogany furniture was faded and worn. Even the curtains flapping alongside each of the four windows had a tired look to them, as if they could hardly stand up to one more ocean breeze.

Having lived all her life in the bustle of modern cities, Bree preferred glass and steel skyscrapers to raggedy old buildings in the middle of nowhere. Still she had to admit this one held a unique appeal. Maybe it was the setting, perched on the spit of land that made up one edge of the harbor. Maybe it was the well-salted local legends Mavis had been relaying for the past hour. Then again, Bree thought as she stifled a yawn, she was so tired from her early flight and long bus ride that anything that wasn't moving looked good to her right now.

Tomorrow morning she'd come to her senses and see this place for what it actually was: a decrepit old tower with a spinning light on top.

At a rare lull in the conversation, Cooper stood. "I hate to do this, ladies, but I'd better get going. I've got a real estate closing at three, and I need to go over my notes."

From her chair upholstered in threadbare needlepoint, Mavis pointed up at him. "You tell your mother I'm still expecting her for bridge on Saturday. I'm not pairing up with any amateur against the Marlowes. They cheat if you don't know what you're doing."

"Yes, ma'am." Turning to Bree, he added, "Your stuff's still in my car. I'll bring it in for you."

Despite her insistence on doing things for herself, this chivalry thing was starting to grow on her, and she was just tired enough to take him up on his offer. Then her brain kicked into gear, reminding her that depending on others to help you gave them a chance to let you down.

Determined not to make that disastrous mistake again, she forced herself to her feet. "I can get it."

"It's not a problem."

"It is for me." For Mavis's benefit, Bree used a sugary voice. But to be sure he didn't misunderstand, she gave him the very stern look she trained on anyone with the gall to make her life difficult. Which was most people, she realized suddenly. That probably explained why she'd perfected that look.

Pushing the uncomfortable revelation aside, she followed him through the kitchen and down the stone steps.

"Something wrong?" he asked as he handed her bags out to her.

"No. Why?"

Turning, he leaned back against the fender and crossed his arms. "That was about the biggest sigh I've ever heard. Look, I know this place isn't what you're used to, but under the circumstances, it's the best I could do."

"Oh, it's not that." A curious dragonfly chose that moment to hover in front of her. Shooing it away, she decided to come clean with the man who'd been so nice to her. "I've got some things to sort out, I guess, and that makes me pensive."

"Professional things or personal things?"

It was absolutely none of his business, and she almost told him so. But his somber expression made it clear he wasn't being nosy, but was actually concerned about her. A complete stranger who'd barreled into town and hijacked his day. It was hard to believe, but here, on the edge of nowhere, she'd come across a truly nice guy. It had been so long since the last one, she'd almost forgotten what they were like.

Shrugging, she admitted, "A little of both."

"And that makes you sigh." When she nodded, he said, "A word of advice?"

"Sure."

After he swung into the driver's seat, he continued, "If you want folks around here to open up to you, don't use words like 'pensive.' It makes you sound like a poet."

Nick had told her pretty much the same thing while critiquing her portfolio, and she couldn't help smiling. "I'll keep that in mind."

"Meantime, I'd like to take you to dinner tonight. I can tell you how the lighthouse got its name."

Bree was fairly certain she'd have that tidbit after another round of tea and gingerbread with Mavis, and she almost said as much. But something made her stop.

It had been a long time since someone had been as kind to her as Cooper had. He was sweet and easy on the eyes, and she wouldn't mind spending the evening with him. She could get some vivid details for her story while enjoying the evening with a handsome man. Where was the harm in that? "That would be great. But I have to warn you, I didn't bring my cocktail dress and high heels."

"That's good, 'cause I was thinking we'd meet the boats at the dock to pick our lobsters, then walk up to The Crow's Nest for dinner."

She'd spent plenty of time in harbor cities all along the East Coast, and she'd eaten tons of fresh seafood. Never had she chosen her own meal, and she doubted any of her dates had even considered asking her to. Apparently Cooper took her slow response for hesitation.

"Unless you'd rather not," he added quickly. "We can order at the restaurant instead."

"Actually I'd like to see the wharf up close. Would the crews mind if I take pictures?"

"Mind?" Laughing, he started the engine. "They'll

be falling all over themselves to see who can impress you the most."

When she heard herself laugh, it almost surprised her. With her life crashing down around her ears, she hadn't done much of that recently, and it felt good. "That sounds like fun."

"How about if I pick you up just before five? They'll all be coming in around then, and you can meet them. You'll find enough characters down there for a whole string of articles."

"That sounds great. I'll see you then."

As he drove away, she watched him with honest appreciation. That he'd devised another way to help with her work touched her in a totally unexpected way. Despite what he knew about her sketchy judgment, Cooper was treating her like a pro. Her confidence was still in tatters, but the respect he was showing her made her think she just might be able to turn the page and start a new chapter in her career.

She certainly hoped so. Because all through college and the past few years, she'd put every ounce of talent and energy she had into her journalism.

Since first learning to write, she'd loved nothing more than spinning stories. As she got older, she discovered she had a knack for describing things she saw and heard, and that people seemed to like talking to her. A well-placed question or two usually got them started, and all she had to do was listen. That, her father informed her, was a valuable skill, and he'd mentored her with great enthusiasm for her growing ability. As she'd progressed from local papers to national coverage of truly important issues, his pride in her had increased. He'd taken her recent fall from grace almost as hard as she had.

For his sake—and her own—she was determined to wrestle her career back on to its upward track. Without it, she was nothing.

Pessimism had gotten to be a nasty habit with her, and she consciously pushed the defeatist thought aside. She'd promised to call her mother when she got settled, so she pulled out her cell phone to check the signal. It wasn't great, but good enough for a quick call, so she thumbed the speed dial for the number.

When her mother answered, Bree put on a smile she hoped would reach through the connection. "Hey there. I'm set at the hotel, so this is me calling you like I promised."

"Thank you, sweetie. I know it's silly, but I appreciate you calling."

"No problem." Bree craned her neck for a look at the mirrored light rotating overhead. "You should see this place, Mom. It's an old lighthouse a stone's throw from the water. Very *Wuthering Heights*."

"It sounds wonderful." An art teacher at a small college in Connecticut, her very creative mother admired anything with character. "Send me some pictures if you have time."

"Hang on." Strolling a few yards away, Bree snapped a photo with her phone and texted it over. It took longer than usual, but it managed to get through. "How's that for service?"

"Oh, it's beautiful! Think of how many ships have sailed past it on their way into the harbor. All the sailors and crewmen, just imagine the stories they could tell."

"I'll be finding out later on." Bree shared her plans for interviewing the fishermen. "It should be good background for the article."

"You like it there, don't you? I can hear it in your voice."

"It's fine." The mayor was especially fine, but she wasn't going there. Mom would get all kinds of romantic notions from that, and Bree didn't need the aggravation of having to fend them off. Completely focused on resurrecting her career, she had no time for distractions, however attractive they might be.

"I have to be honest," she continued, "I didn't think much of the town 'til I saw the lighthouse. You'd love Mavis Freeman. She's been running things since her husband died three years ago, but they still call her the keeper's widow. The house is full of antiques, including her, and I'm convinced she's memorized the history of every ship that ever went by."

"You've got a love of the sea running through your blood. I'm not sure you remember, but one of my ancestors was a sea captain. Seamus O'Connell was his name."

"I researched him. He was a pirate, and when the British finally caught him, they hanged him."

"That may be true, but he still loved the sea. I'm sure that's where you get it from."

Thankfully, a beep alerted Bree that she had another call. When she checked the ID, her heart tripped over itself with the alarming combination of excitement and dread that had become all too familiar lately. "My editor's trying to reach me, Mom. I'll call you in the morning."

"I'll be here!"

Bree said goodbye and switched over to the other call. "Hello, Nick. What can I do for you?"

"Just making sure you got up there in one piece."

Her intuition was sizzling, which meant there was more to this call than a simple check-in. Not long ago she'd have confronted him directly, but these days she was playing things a little closer to the vest. If she'd done that before, she'd still be working at her dream job in Boston.

She wasn't thrilled about being flung so far down the ladder, and hopefully being more reserved would keep her from tumbling out of the business altogether. "My connecting flight was delayed, and the bus took a while, but I got here around noon."

"Good. How's everyone treating you?"

"Very well, thanks." While she could tell he was fishing, she had no idea what he was angling for. "Is there anything in particular you want me to include in my article?"

"Lots of local color, anything unique that catches your eye. You're not from there, so you should be able to pick up on things that'll appeal to visitors. I want you to paint a great picture of Holiday Harbor so our readers can't wait to book a ticket up there."

After getting a few more similarly vague instructions, it dawned on Bree that her questions were too subtle. Despite her vow to be more reserved, she broke down and went the direct route. "What am I really doing here? I mean, it's quaint and charming and all, but 'sleepy little town' is an understatement. The best article in the world won't change that, and I can't see why you'd pay me to come all this way to write about this place."

"Cooper didn't tell you?"

"Only that you grew up here."

Nick chuckled. "Yes, I graduated a couple years after Cooper. He tutored me for a while, and without him I never would've gotten accepted at New York University. Anyway, when he asked me if *Kaleidscope* could do the town a favor, I was happy to help. We do have a national audience these days, you know."

Nick had a reputation for being tightfisted, and she'd picked up on something totally unlike him. "So they're not paying you to promote Holiday Harbor?"

"Nope."

Nick had hired her to do a story that wouldn't financially benefit his business? To her, that was a foreign concept. "That's generous of you."

"Hey, we do what we can, y'know?"

Actually, she didn't know. She couldn't remember the last time she'd met someone she honestly admired, but it seemed her prospective new boss fell into that category. She heard a smothering sound, then Nick's voice came back full volume. "There's a problem with tomorrow's layout, so I have to run. Do a stellar job on this, Bree. There's a lot of good people counting on you."

The line went dead, and Bree shut her own phone off. Tapping it against her chin, she gazed out at the water, lulled by the rhythm of the waves crashing on the rocks. The sun played over the spray, forming minirainbows here and there in the mist. With the weathered lighthouse as a backdrop, it was a remarkable sight.

In spite of her earlier skepticism, Bree reflected on the possibility that her mother could be right. Maybe the old pirate's love of the ocean was getting to her after all.

Chapter Three

On his way back out to the lighthouse later that afternoon, Cooper congratulated himself on a successful residential closing. Granddad had always handled those, so Cooper hadn't done one in a while. Fortunately the two real estate agents knew their stuff, and all he'd had to do was dot the i's and cross the t's for his client. Before long another young family would be calling Holiday Harbor home. It was a great way to end what had become an interesting day.

Bree Farrell fascinated him. At a young age he'd learned to read people, mostly by shutting up and listening to them talk. During long days on the water Granddad had taught him to watch the fish closely, reading their movements to predict where they were headed. You could do the same with people, he'd explained, interpreting their body language as well as their words to get a clear picture of how they actually felt. That skill came in handy when their behavior contradicted what they were saying.

Based on what he'd seen so far, Bree was fighting a bigger battle than she was admitting to. Despite her bravado, he saw the uncertainty in her dark eyes, muting the spark of intelligence that managed to snap through frequently enough to intrigue him. Fortunately she'd be leaving soon. All he had to do was get through the Fourth, and she'd be on her way back to Richmond.

It was better that way, he knew. He'd once gotten in way too deep with a woman committed to her career, and her rejection of his marriage proposal still stung. He had no intention of making the same mistake again.

As he pulled in at the lighthouse, he shoved those old regrets to the back of his mind. Someday, when he finally had time to get back into the dating scene, it would be with someone down-to-earth who loved the ocean as much as he did.

When he got to the end of the drive, he was surprised to find Bree waiting for him on the front stoop. He was even more surprised to see her scratching Reggie behind his ears, while the little pig grunted in delight.

"That's not something you see every day," Cooper teased as he stepped down.

Eyes twinkling with humor, she pointed a threatening finger at him. "If you tell a single soul I like this little oinker, I'll sue you for defamation of character."

"Don't worry. Your secret's safe with me."

"You're a lawyer. Don't you lie for a living?"

He knew she was joking, but her accusation brought up more memories he'd rather leave buried in the past. Reminding himself she had no way of knowing that, he took a deep breath and let it go. "Never to pretty ladies sitting on porches. Besides, it's not your fault. Reggie's a shameless flirt."

"He sure is."

Chucking him under the chin, she made kissing

noises but stopped short of actually delivering one. Obviously smitten, the pig closed his eyes and gave her his version of a smile, wagging his tail for good measure. It was one of the cutest things Cooper had ever seen. He'd take a picture, but he suspected Bree would toss his phone in the water to destroy the evidence. Still it was oddly comforting to know there was a soft heart under all that bluster. Recalling his earlier musings about the pretty reporter, he firmly put the brakes on that train of thought. She was here to do a job, and that was it. With a sharp mind and a tongue to match, she was the kind of woman who could drive a man crazy with no effort at all.

"The crews should be coming in about now," he said. "Are you ready to go?"

"Definitely."

As she shouldered her camera bag and stood up, the breeze ruffled through the long curls she'd left loose around her shoulders. She was dressed head to toe in black like a pint-size burglar, and he couldn't help grinning. While full-on black might be appropriate for life in Richmond, here she'd stand out like a sore thumb.

Apparently he was staring a little too intently, because she frowned and glanced down at her trousers. "Am I covered in pig hair or something?"

"No. Why?"

"Usually when people grin like that, they're making fun."

She didn't say "of me," but Cooper easily filled in the blank. Seeing the hesitance in her eyes, he wouldn't even think of suggesting she change her clothes. So she'd stand out. So what? With her striking looks and fearless demeanor, he had the feeling she'd turn heads no matter what she was wearing.

"Not me," he assured her. "I'm looking forward to spending the evening with you, so I smiled. I promise not to do it again."

A grateful smile brightened her features, transforming them with the pixie look he'd glimpsed earlier when she'd briefly let down her guard. It made her seem much younger, and he could envision her as a fresh-faced journalist, eager to take on the world before it turned against her. What had she been like back then? he wondered.

Realizing he'd ventured into dangerous territory, he pushed the emotion aside and smiled as he motioned her toward the car. "After you."

"Why did you put the top and doors back on?" she asked when he opened the passenger side for her.

"Earlier today I got the feeling you didn't appreciate the open-air look."

"You didn't have to do this for me. I'm not that picky."

Did anyone ever go out of their way for her? Cooper wondered as he started the engine. His guess would be no, which explained her fierce independent streak. Being a lifelong New Englander, he'd always admired self-reliance. But for some reason thinking that Bree had no choice other than to fend for herself really bothered him.

Shrugging it off, he headed for the wharf. "I talked to some of the captains, and they're thrilled that you're coming down."

"I wish you hadn't done that. I prefer to do candid interviews."

"Trust me," Cooper told her with a chuckle. "These guys have been out on the water for twelve hours. You're better off giving them a chance to clean up a little before you meet them."

After a moment she admitted, "Okay. That makes sense."

While they chatted about nothing in particular, Cooper's opinion of her continued to improve. Her queries were thoughtful and out of the box, and she asked things most visitors didn't consider important. Were the crews local or from elsewhere? Full-time or day laborers? Were the docks maintained by the town or the county? How many women worked on the crews?

With each question she asked him, his confidence in her abilities grew. Many in town—himself included—had questioned the wisdom of promoting Holiday Harbor to random outsiders. Their debate had revolved around the best way to accomplish their goals without being viewed as a joke or a tourist trap.

Cooper was now convinced that Bree was perfect for the job. It didn't take a genius to figure out she had something to prove, not only to her editor, but to herself. He sensed that she'd do whatever it took to write an exceptional article and show Nick she could handle any challenge he wanted to throw at her.

Cooper was only too glad to help her do it.

When they arrived at the busy waterfront, every boat, from two-man skiff to commercial lobster boat, was tied up in port. Judging by the relative cleanliness of the crews, the captains had passed Cooper's message along over their radios and ordered everyone to clean up before coming ashore. They wouldn't pass muster for a night at the Metropolitan Opera, but they'd all made an effort to spiff up after their long, grueling day.

As he and Bree made their way down the ramp, she pulled a steno pad and pen out of the front pocket of her camera bag.

Cooper chuckled. "Going old school, huh?"

"Some people don't trust technology." Casting a glance down the dock, she smiled. "I'm guessing these guys will feel more comfortable with me if I take notes the old-fashioned way."

When they reached the landing, he stopped her with a hand on her arm. "Hang on a minute."

She opened her mouth to say something just as one of the veteran crewmen announced, "Off with your hats, fellas."

They all removed their caps, lowering their heads as he continued. "Heavenly Father, we thank You for a beautiful day free of breakdowns and injuries. We pray the catch in our holds brings us a good price so we can afford to keep working the sea we love. In Your name we pray. Amen."

Cooper echoed the sentiment and caught Bree's look of surprise from the corner of his eye. "Something wrong?"

"No, I just didn't expect to hear a sermon on the dock."

"Their jobs are incredibly dangerous," he explained patiently. "It's important for them to know they're not alone out there on the water."

Still looking perplexed, she let the subject drop, and he stepped back to give her the spotlight. While she introduced herself to the fishermen, he marveled again at her ability to make people feel at ease. Everyone but him, it seemed. Unfortunately he still hadn't figured out why.

"So tell me," Bree addressed the oldest captain, a sixty-something old salt fondly referred to as Cap'n Jack. "What's the biggest threat to your business these days?"

"Them over there." Nodding toward a chartered fishing yacht, he scowled. "These rich guys plow into our fishing lanes and scare off half the catch. They just want to come back with something to stuff and mount over the fireplace in their den. But this is how we make our living and take care of our families."

She cocked her head as if considering her response, but Cooper wouldn't be surprised to learn she had most of her questions memorized. "They spend money here in town, though, at the hotels and restaurants. If they stop coming, how would you replace it?"

"Dunno." His leathery face cracked into a scowl he aimed in Cooper's direction. "Ask our new mayor."

"You don't approve of the job Mayor Landry's doing?"

"No, missy, I don't. Nothing against Cooper, o'course," he added in a grudging half apology. "It's just I don't see the need to change things that've been workin' the way they are for generations."

There was some grumbled agreement, and Cooper carefully kept his expression neutral. All these men liked him well enough, but to them he was still wet behind the ears and in need of seasoning. The fact that Granddad was gone had no bearing on their opinions. They wanted the judge, and barring that, they wanted the town to continue running the way he'd done it for the past twenty years. Period, end of story.

"Aw, lay off, Jack," one of his crew members chided. "Cooper ain't like most college boys. He's done his time out on the water."

Bree turned to Cooper with undisguised astonishment. "You worked a fishing boat?"

"My uncle was a lobsterman. I worked with him in the summers when I got old enough."

"Tough job," she commented, then turned back to the crews. "I lived in Boston for a while, so I've got real respect for how hard you all work."

"Boston." One of the younger hands spat into the water. "Their winter's got nothin' on ours. In the spring we gotta chop a path through the ice just to get to the fish."

Grinning, Bree jotted a note on her pad. While the others chimed in with their own tales, the interview devolved into general boasting. Then she did the worst thing possible.

"Can I get some pictures of you guys?"

Shouting agreement, they pushed and shoved to be in front. Finally Jack hollered for them all to knock it off and waded into the mix to sort them by height. While they got organized, Bree glanced over at Cooper and gave him a little wink, which told him she knew exactly what she was doing. Who'd have thought their very intense visitor had a playful streak? Cooper mused with a grin. She had these rough-and-tumble men right where she wanted them, playing up to her, falling all over themselves to give her unusual personal details for her article.

And photos? What man didn't want a pretty woman taking his picture, telling him it just might wind up on the internet?

"Grab that camera, lawyer boy!" Jack called out. "We want a picture with the little lady."

Shaking his head, Cooper grinned and took the 35mm

from her. Then he waited while they did rock-paper-scissors to decide who got to stand next to her. As he focused in, he marveled at how quickly she'd gotten them all eating out of the palm of her hand.

If she was like this with men in general, he pitied the one who actually fell in love with her someday. The poor guy wouldn't stand a chance.

Once she and Cooper had chosen their lobsters, Bree followed him up the metal gangplank, away from the commercial docks humming with activity. It was pretty warm, and the smell of fresh fish and seaweed permeated the salt-laden breeze.

Oh, her mother would love that one, she thought, scribbling it down. It was poetic and earthy at the same time, just like Mom. With seagulls circling overhead, the bustling port looked busy enough to support five towns.

Until she noticed the other side.

The far end of the U-shaped dock was completely empty. No boats, no people, even the access gate had been welded shut. Some of the wooden deck boards were missing, and algae covered the lower areas of everything that remained.

"How long has it been that way?" she asked, motioning toward the abandoned section.

"Five years, give or take. It got to be so expensive to maintain, the town council voted to close it down and save the money."

It looked lonely and unwanted, tangible proof of the decline Cooper had described to her earlier. Now she understood his eagerness to entice tourists into the area. He didn't want the rest of his hometown to end up like this.

"Are you okay?" he asked, his brow wrinkling with concern.

She'd been in lots of places that had seen better days, but she'd always managed to keep her professional distance. For some reason this old fishing village was different, and she'd need to put in more effort to remain objective. "Fine. Just hungry."

"Then I guess it's a good thing we're here."

Angling her away from the depressing scene, he motioned her ahead of him through a glass door etched with the Holiday Harbor logo and The Crow's Nest beneath it in flowing script.

"Nice touch, using the same artwork." Noting the familiar design from his shirt, she tapped it on her way through. "Visitors pick up on things like that."

"That's the general idea. Hi, Frances."

"Cooper. I didn't know you were coming in tonight."

"Neither did I. Do you have a table on the deck?"

"For you? Always," she gushed, giving Bree a suspicious once-over. "And who is this?"

"I'm sorry. Bree Farrell, Frances Cook. Bree came up from Richmond to do an article on Holiday Harbor."

"Cooper!" a man yelled, hurrying over to clap him on the shoulder. Tie askew, he was wearing a button-down and suit jacket with a Vote for Derek! button done up in red, white and blue. Turning to Bree, he offered his hand. "Derek Timms. Cooper and I grew up here and then went to Yale Law together. Since he's practicing here, I just opened my own firm in Oakbridge. I don't know how this goofball does it, but he always manages to show up with the prettiest girl in the place."

"She's not my date, you moron. She's a reporter." He

flipped the outrageous button with his finger. "And she can't vote for you, so just can the speech."

"What are you running for?" Bree asked.

"Mayor." When she flashed Cooper a baffled look, Derek laughed. "Cooper may be allergic to power, but I'm not. We see things the same way, so except for the fact that I'm a much better dresser, the town probably won't even notice the difference."

Cooper chuckled in apparent agreement. "Just as long as you keep those greedy developers outta here, I'll be happy."

After a quick salute, Derek said, "Otter can't make it for golf next Friday, so we've got a spot. Whattya say?"

"Otter?" Bree echoed with a grin. "Is he a really good swimmer or something?"

"Or something," Cooper answered with a grin of his own before focusing on his friend. "Where are you guys playing?"

"Deer Run, the new club over in Oakbridge. Longest course within a hundred miles. You can try out that fancy new driver your mom got you for your birthday."

The two men began discussing various aspects of the new course, leaving Bree at the mercy of Frances. Wonderful.

"A real-live reporter, all the way up here. How about that?" the young woman commented through a frigid smile. "What do you think of our little town?"

"I haven't seen much, but the people I've met so far are fantastic." She added a little bite to her tone to let her know she might be able to fool a nice guy like Cooper, but Bree had her number.

"Sorry about that," Cooper apologized to Bree as

Derek headed back to his table. "But it's impossible to get a tee time at that new club."

For the hostess's benefit, Bree smiled. "No problem."

Frances escorted them to a secluded table on the deck overlooking the bay. Because he was pulling out Bree's chair, he didn't notice the longing look Frances tossed back over her shoulder as she left. Bree could hardly blame her. Even in Richmond Cooper would be considered quite the catch. With so little competition up here, he must look like a prince.

Once they were settled, he crossed his arms on the table. "The crews really warmed up to you, didn't they?"

Taking a sip of her water, she replied, "They were awesome. And very entertaining. It's easy to see how much they love this place."

He cocked his head with a knowing look. "But you don't share their opinion."

She didn't, but Bree wisely refrained from admitting it outright. "I just got here, so I haven't formed an opinion yet."

"How 'bout a gut feel? I won't hold you to it or anything, just curious."

She'd learned the hard way not to voice her impressions, first or otherwise. But his genuine kindness had put some of those usual fears to rest, and she instinctively knew she could trust him. "I love the lighthouse. It's really beautiful out there."

Judging by his bright grin, she'd hit one of his favorite buttons. "Yeah, it is. *Kaleidoscope* has over a million readers nationwide, and I'm hoping we can get enough coverage that people will start to recognize the name and want to come check things out."

"That's my goal, too." She'd meant every word, but

his wary look made her think he didn't believe her. "Did I say something wrong?"

He hesitated, clearly debating whether to start something with her. They didn't know each other well, and she wondered just how much backbone this small-town mayor had under that neatly pressed blue oxford shirt.

Leaning in, his eyes darkened to a murky color that warned her a storm was coming. "Let's get one thing straight right now. I know you're here to rescue your career from the trash heap. I also know this is the last spot on earth you want to be. So let's not pretend you came because Holiday Harbor fascinates you and you're thrilled with this assignment."

Narrowing her eyes, she angled closer just to show him she wasn't intimidated. She seldom went toe-to-toe with such a worthy opponent, and she relished the opportunity. "Fair enough. Since we're being so honest, tell me why you really came back to a town so small, you need a magnifying glass to find it on a map."

A waitress headed their way, and they both eased back to create a more sociable appearance. She took their appetizer order, casting several admiring looks at Cooper before strolling back inside.

"Sickening," Bree groused. "Does every woman within five miles have a thing for you?"

"Actually the older ones prefer my Uncle Joe."

He said it with a completely straight face, and she had to laugh. "You must have killed in the courtroom. I'm usually good at reading people, and I couldn't tell you were joking."

"I wasn't." Taking a sip of water, he set it down and began. "Anyway, like I told you earlier, after Yale I worked at a big firm in New York. Lots of cases, high-profile clients, all the trimmings."

Not all of it had been good, she deduced from his shifting expressions. Watching him tell it was even better than digging it up online. "And you dated—let me guess—an actress."

"A model." His mouth quirked into a cute half grin. "I was almost engaged to Felicia."

"*The* Felicia?" When he nodded, she clapped quietly. "Very nice. But you said 'almost.' What happened?"

"I had a major court case that went on forever. Long story short, we won, and my client was thrilled with the result." He paused, waiting until the waitress set down their crab cakes and informed them their lobsters would be out shortly. Once she was gone, he continued. "Then the moron told me I'd had a little help winning the case."

Bree leaned in. "From the judge?"

Cooper shook his head. "From my client. Apparently, he didn't tell me everything, just what he felt I needed to know to get him acquitted."

"He lied to you?"

"Withheld key facts," Cooper corrected her with a grimace. "Since it was a complex financial issue, the details might not have mattered to the jury, but they mattered to me. I'd faced that kind of thing a few times before, but this time I couldn't rationalize it away. The next day I quit my job and asked Felicia to come back here and marry me."

Bree made a show of looking around. "Not exactly nirvana for models."

"No, but I thought she loved me and wanted to be my wife." Another grimace. "Turned out she loved New York more."

A few choice words came to mind, but Bree kept them to herself. He'd loved the woman enough to marry her after all. It wouldn't make him feel any better if Bree insulted the self-centered twit, even if she totally deserved it.

"Now it's your turn," Cooper said, popping half a crab cake into his mouth. "Should I be worried about some jealous boyfriend coming to beat me up for taking you out to dinner?"

"You might," she said in between bites. "If I had one."

"You're kidding." When she shook her head, he stared at her like she'd just beamed in from another galaxy. "How does that happen to someone as pretty as you?"

Since the man had been engaged to one of *People* magazine's Most Beautiful Women, and had a very dry wit besides, Bree wasn't sure she should take him seriously. But his stunned demeanor never changed, and she decided he was playing it straight this time.

"I'm too busy," she said simply. When he cocked his head in disbelief, she figured that since he'd been up front with her, she owed him the truth. "Even if I wasn't, my parents' messy divorce convinced me that constant traveling and marriage don't mix."

Cooper absorbed it with a somber expression. "I'm sorry to hear that."

"Don't be. I was in college when they finally split, and to be honest, it was a relief. My dad was an AP correspondent, and we moved around a lot. When he was on assignment, they fought about him being away too much. When he was home, they fought about him being underfoot. Not the best model for happily ever after."

"I guess not." After a sip of water, he asked, "Which one of them came up with your unique name?"

Bree groaned. "My mother. She's a hopeless romantic, and her favorite movie is *Sabrina*. You know, the one where the two rich brothers fall in love with the butler's daughter who used to be a plain Jane and—poof!—turns into Audrey Hepburn?"

Grinning, Cooper forked up a cherry tomato from his salad. "Sounds familiar."

"As if that wasn't mortifying enough, she saddled me with Constance for a middle name. It's a tribute to some aunt she adored, but really, who uses names like that anymore?"

He laughed, and even though it was at her expense, she couldn't help joining in. There was something about him that made her feel at ease, as if he'd pushed some invisible "relax" button inside her that no one else had ever found. While they devoured their lobsters, they chatted comfortably about nothing in particular. Before long, it felt as if they'd known each other for years instead of only a few hours.

For dessert they ordered a humongous slice of Boston cream pie and two forks. It was like a scene from some gushy romantic movie, but Bree was having such a great time, she decided to ignore the sappiness and just enjoy the evening.

They'd nearly finished off their pie when he said, "I almost forgot to tell you how the lighthouse got its name."

Actually Mavis already had, but Bree decided to let him have his moment. "That's right. Go ahead."

"After a dozen ships or so broke up on those rocks, the townsfolk got together and built the tower. They called it Last Chance because it was the captains' last chance to correct their course before running aground."

"Neat story," she murmured, scribbling it down even though she'd recorded Mavis telling it earlier. Normally she wouldn't humor a source this way, but Cooper had been so great with her, she didn't want to hurt his feelings.

"So, that's it." Setting down his dessert fork, he checked his watch. "I guess I should get you back, then."

It had been a long, exhausting day, and she was definitely ready to hit the sack. But when she opened her mouth to agree, she heard herself say, "If you've got time, I wouldn't mind hearing some more about the summer-long regatta."

What? Where had that come from? Betrayed by her suddenly unpredictable emotions, Bree forced herself to smile as if she hadn't completely lost her mind.

Fortunately Cooper either didn't notice her momentary lapse of sanity or he was so accustomed to odd characters it didn't bother him. "Sure. What do you want to know?"

"Whatever you think people who aren't from around here would find interesting. Quirky," she clarified, pulling her steno pad over to take notes. "Like what kind of costume does Reggie wear?"

Threading his fingers together on the table, Cooper grinned. "He's always Teddy Roosevelt. Even wears little glasses and a forest ranger's hat."

"Who does Mavis go as?"

"Mavis. She doesn't think much of dressing up herself, but she's got no reservations about decking out Reggie. She says he enjoys pretending to be someone else once in a while."

Laughing, Bree jotted that down and set up her phone to record. If this first nugget was any indication, she was in for some Holiday Harbor gold.

Chapter Four

Cooper had neglected to tell Bree the tan hatchback he'd borrowed for her was a standard. Shifting wasn't her favorite thing to do at seven in the morning, and she ground her teeth along with the transmission. She vaguely recalled learning the basic concepts in high school, but stalled it several times before getting the hang of the clutch and shifter. Mavis paused in her laundry hanging to watch, and while Bree couldn't hear anything, in the side mirror she saw the woman laughing at her.

Ignoring her, Bree finally slid the little car into gear, working the pedals to keep it running while she gradually built up speed. It was fortunate she didn't have to use the highway, she thought as she drove up over the ridge and headed for town. She would've gotten a ticket for impeding traffic.

On Main Street the sleepy village had already come to life. Cars and pickups were lined up in the diagonal parking spots, and she had to park a good distance from the business district. Glancing toward the docks, she noticed those lots were full up, and the fleet of fishing vessels was gone. Every pier post was occupied by a seagull, snoozing while they waited for the boats to come back and toss out something for them to eat.

Since there wouldn't be much activity down there for a while, Bree set her sights on what was going on in town. Cooper's law office was closed, but she was surprised to find the neighboring door wide open. Brown paper covered the huge display windows, but classical music was playing inside. Taking a shot, she strolled in, hoping to find someone interesting to talk to.

The ceilings had to be fourteen feet high, and judging by the built-in shelving that ringed the open space, the building had once been a general store. The hardwood floors and trim had been recently sanded, with several patches of different stains scattered here and there. An archway led into a dark hallway at the back, and a carved door marked Private obviously led upstairs to offices or an apartment. It was pretty rough now, but it didn't take much imagination to see how it would look when everything was restored to its former character-filled glory.

"Hello?" Bree's voice echoed through the cavernous room, and she heard footsteps in the hallway.

When the shop's owner appeared, Bree almost swallowed her tongue. The gorgeous blonde dressed for a casual day at the country club could be only one person. "Whoa," she breathed. "You're Julia Stanton."

Irritation flashed through the woman's blue eyes before she masked it with a smile. "Yes. May I help you?"

What a coup this was. The daughter of Ambassador Frederick Stanton had disappeared from public life nearly a year ago, and the various media had tried to locate her, without success. Neglecting her recent vow to be more circumspect about things, Bree blurted out, "What are you doing here?"

"Renovating my building. What are *you* doing here?"

"Looking for someone to talk to. People get up and going pretty early around here."

"We like to make the most of the day." She eyed Bree's steno pad like it was a pit viper. "I don't speak to reporters."

"Sorry." Bree shoved the pad into her bag and offered her hand. "Bree Farrell. I'm doing a story on Holiday Harbor for *Kaleidoscope* magazine."

That got her a frosty look. "So I've heard."

Before the woman had a chance to boot her onto the sidewalk, Bree rushed ahead. "As a new resident, I'd love to get your take on the town. No names, I promise."

Julia gave her a dubious look. "I've never had much success with reporters keeping promises."

"That's not how I operate." Hoping to convince her, Bree added, "Do you have time for coffee? We can chat for a few minutes, and if you don't like what I have to say, I'll pretend I never met you."

Julia hesitated, glancing around while she considered Bree's offer. Clearly she was trying not to be rude, a skill she'd mastered while traveling the world as part of the U.S. Diplomatic Corps. Finally she met Bree's gaze and said, "I've got coffee made already, but it's pretty dusty in here. We can sit outside and talk, if you want."

Bree had anticipated a flat-out no. Before Julia could change her mind, Bree agreed and headed for the door. Outside she ran into Derek Timms. Literally.

"Oh, man," he said as he reached out to steady her. "I'm sorry. Are you okay?"

"It was my fault," she assured him with a laugh. "I wasn't paying attention."

He gave her the same broad friendly smile she'd gotten last night. Only now, in the sunlight, she noticed the gesture didn't light up his eyes the way Cooper's did. It had a practiced quality to it, as if he'd rehearsed so he could pull it out at a moment's notice. She wasn't sure what that meant, if anything, but she tucked the observation into her rapidly growing mental file.

Leaning back against a sporty red convertible parked at the curb, he said, "You look like you're in a hurry. Can I give you a lift somewhere?"

The move plainly said, "This is my cool toy," and she fought the urge to roll her eyes at his subtle boasting. "I'm just waiting for someone. Thanks, though."

"A source? That's what you journalists call them, right?"

He knew the answer to that, but for some reason he was pretending otherwise to get on her good side. Bree got the feeling he was well acquainted with how egos worked, since he seemed to have a healthy one of his own.

"That's what we call them, all right," she said as Julia glided up beside her. Including her in the conversation, Bree took the coffee Julia offered her with a smile. "But this one I just call 'local shop owner.'"

"Our Julia doesn't talk to the press," he warned, flashing the lady in question an appreciative look. "We like having her all to ourselves."

The warm atmosphere cooled slightly, but Julia's gracious smile never faltered. "Thank you for the compliment, Derek. When you see Frances, please give her my best."

That dampened his chipper mood, and he quickly disengaged from their conversation. After handing each of them a Vote for Derek! button, he got into his car and sped away.

"Were you talking about Frances Cook?" Bree asked quietly as she and Julia settled on a wrought-iron bench under the blue awning. The scent of vanilla and something more exotic drifted from their mugs, and she took a long delicious swallow. It tasted even better than it smelled.

"I'm not one for gossip." Julia paused for a sip of coffee. "But I've seen them together, and she obviously adores him. I'm sure he's harmless, but I don't want to encourage his flirting when she seems to have her heart set on him."

Derek was handsome and funny, and there was no question he had the Prince Charming routine down pat. Still Bree couldn't for the life of her comprehend why any woman would put up with his roaming eye. Fortunately she managed not to say so. Instead she went with a noncommittal, "Huh. That's interesting."

Julia gave her a sharp look, then seemed to catch on and shifted to a knowing smile. "That's your way of stalling, isn't it? A response that doesn't say anything, but keeps the discussion moving."

Bree was impressed. Apparently, there was a lot more to Julia Stanton than Hollywood goddess looks and a bottomless bank account. "You seem to know a lot about my business." Glancing backward at the blank storefront, she added, "I'd love to know more about yours."

"Such as?"

"This is such a beautiful old building. What's it going to be?"

The practiced expression gave way to excitement, and her eyes danced with enthusiasm. "A toy store."

"Really? In this economy, isn't that kind of risky? I mean, how do you plan to compete with the big discount stores?"

"By offering things they don't even know exist," Julia replied proudly. "I'll stock unique toys from all over the world, but for prices everyone can afford. The things they buy at Toyland will be their children's favorites, and I'll be the only one providing them."

"A niche market," Bree said, nodding to show she understood. "Very smart."

"Thank you."

Smiling, Julia leaned back and crossed one long elegant leg over the other. It was a movie star pose, and Bree was dying to snap a picture. But she'd made a promise to protect Julia's privacy, and she wouldn't dream of breaking it.

Completely by accident she'd stumbled across a woman who was neither her professional competition nor a rival for some guy's attention. In her experience women like that were so rare, she could count her female friends on one hand.

It was too bad she'd be in town for such a short time, Bree thought wistfully. Under different circumstances she and Julia probably would have become friends.

"So, how was your morning?" Cooper asked when he connected with Bree outside his office early Friday afternoon.

"Great." As she settled into the passenger seat, she added, "I met Julia Stanton, and we had a great time together. I even helped her do some work in her shop."

"Funny, you didn't strike me as the handy, do-it-yourself type."

"I'm no contractor, but I'm perfectly capable of tearing down layers of old wallpaper," she informed him airily. "That car you loaned me is another story."

She gave him a wry smile, and he chuckled. "Sorry about that. All the rental companies were sold out."

"It took me a while, but I remembered my driver's ed lessons before I completely shredded the transmission. Mavis just about died laughing, though."

"No doubt." Tapping the to-go cups in the console, he nodded at the bag sitting on the dash. "I didn't know what you'd like for lunch, so I brought a bunch of different sandwiches. Help yourself."

Rustling through the bag, she took out a ham and cheese croissant and washed down a bite of it with her soda. "On the phone you wouldn't tell me anything about where we're going. It must be important for you to go all James Bond on me."

He'd done that on purpose. In a few short hours he'd picked up on the fact that Bree was a visual person, and she responded best to what she saw for herself. But now that he'd piqued her curiosity, he figured it wouldn't hurt to give her some background. "There's a place down the coast called Sandy Cove. It's been abandoned for a couple years now, and I think exploring it will help you with your article. Y'know, a real-life example of what could happen if we don't do something, and soon."

"Great idea." Downing the last of her lunch in one mouthful, she fished out her tablet and stylus. "When was Sandy Cove founded?"

Cooper swerved around some geese waddling across the road, then continued around the curve. "Five years after Holiday Harbor. A few families liked the spot and decided to make a home there. Same history as ours, for the most part."

"Which is why you're so worried."

He heard genuine sympathy in her tone. When he glanced over, he found her wearing the same troubled expression she'd had last night, staring at the decommissioned town dock. There were more layers to their guest than he'd expected, and he had to admit she was starting to grow on him.

Bad, he cautioned himself. Very, very bad. Losing Felicia had cost him a big chunk of his heart, and he still hadn't fully recovered. He wasn't ready for anything beyond casual acquaintances with women. Especially not one who'd made it clear she was bolting as soon as she typed "The End."

Attraction was one thing, he reasoned, and there was nothing he could do about that. But acting on it was completely within his control, and he had no intention of setting himself up for a heartbreaking fall like the one he'd taken with Felicia. His legal colleagues in New York hadn't dubbed him the Ice Man for nothing. He was well aware he'd been repeating the same basic warning to himself since Bree had stepped off the bus. This time he meant it.

With that decision firmly made, he dragged his attention back to the road and Bree's running commentary.

"...and there's Reggie, lying next to me, staring at me like a dog waiting for me to take him on his morning walk. Mavis conveniently forgot to tell me he likes the bed in my room. For the life of me I still can't figure out how he climbed all those stairs up to the tower and opened the door."

Cooper laughed at the vivid picture she'd created in his mind. "He's pretty clever, and spoiled besides. Mavis and Henry never had children, but she loves animals. I think that's why they like her so much."

"So do you." Bree pulled her whirling hair over her shoulder and started braiding it to keep it in place. "And in spite of the fact that she talks to you as if you're ten, she seems to like you, too."

"There's a story there, if you're interested."

He could almost feel her ears perk up as she swiveled inside the seat belt to face him. "Always. I love a good story."

"It's the Irish in you. You're probably descended from a long line of Celtic bards."

She laughed, a bright, heartwarming sound he wouldn't mind hearing more often. "What does a Yale attorney know about Celtic bards?"

"You'd be surprised."

"No doubt. But I'm actually descended from a long line of Irish stowaways. One of my mom's ancestors even became captain of his own ship. The hard way."

"A pirate?" When she nodded, he let out a low whistle. "Guess I'll have to watch my step or you'll make me walk the plank."

She answered with a fairly convincing pirate's growl. "Got that right. Now, what about your Mavis story?"

"She never paid much attention to me when I was a kid. Then one afternoon when I was about twelve or so, I was on the bay with my old sailboat, trying to figure out how to work the sails with the wind. She was in their yard and came to stand on the point and yell at me for being so clumsy. I was frustrated, so I yelled something back, and she stood there scowling at me."

"I can just imagine what you said," Bree commented with a grin.

"It wasn't very nice. Anyway, I guess she took pity on me, 'cause she talked me through tacking into the wind and helped me get back to shore. I really appreciated her help, so the next day I got up the guts to take her a bouquet of flowers." Pausing, he chuckled at the memory. "She was so grateful, you'd have thought I brought her the crown jewels. She, Henry and I ended up talking most of the afternoon and ever since then, she's been one of my favorite people."

"She must get lonely out there, all by herself."

The softness in Bree's voice told him she understood being alone, feeling as if no one cared about you. Cooper's inborn protectiveness started rustling just below the surface, and in self-defense, he firmly pushed it back down. "Like she said yesterday, she's not much for people. But someone goes out there every day for one reason or another, making sure everything's okay. I live just across the harbor, so a lot of times it's me."

"You guys check on her without letting her know you're checking on her," Bree commented with a smile. "That's so sweet."

"That's what folks do."

"Not the ones I know."

"Then you've been hanging out with the wrong kind of people." When she laughed again, he glanced over at her. "What's so funny?"

"You sound like my dad. 'Surround yourself with good people, Bree. They'll make or break you.'"

"Sounds like my kinda guy."

"Except for my mom, he's everyone's kinda guy," she said proudly. "I wish I was more like him."

"I don't know," Cooper replied as they passed the faded sign welcoming them to Sandy Cove. "From what I saw last night, our entire fishing fleet is half in love with you already. Those guys are notoriously suspicious, so that has to be some kind of record."

"Yeah, men seem to warm up to me quicker than women do."

He grinned over at her. "I don't doubt that for a second."

Making a sour face, she pulled out her camera. "Could you stop for a minute so I can get some pics?"

"Sure."

He pulled over to the side and shifted into Park. While she lined up her shots, he was struck by the contradictions in her personality. When she was working, she came off as confident, almost cocky. But when it came to anything remotely personal, she had the demeanor of a teenage girl trying to figure out how to make people like her. While he admired her professionalism, that sliver of vulnerability gave her a softer, more feminine appeal.

When she sat down and smiled over at him, his stomach did a disconcerting flip. Impossible as it had seemed at their first meeting, he liked her. And that could only lead to trouble.

Then again it wasn't her fault he was still gun-shy when it came to women, so he smiled back. "All set?"

"Yeah. Thanks."

"No problem." Pulling back onto the deserted road, he asked, "Do you prefer writing or photography?"

"I enjoy both." Tossing her braid over her shoulder, she thumbed through the shots on her screen. "Working for *Kaleidoscope* is the first time I've gotten to do my own stills, and it's really fun. The photos are like extra notes for later and since I'm the only one here, Nick will be using a couple for the article."

"So you get all the credit," Cooper filled in the obvious blank. "And a little extra cash, besides."

"What's wrong with that?"

There was the flinty no-nonsense side of her again. His rosy image of her warming up to him—and his town—evaporated like the morning mist offshore. He should have been relieved, but for some reason he was disappointed. Trying to shake it off, he shrugged. "Nothing. It's natural to want to get paid as much as you can."

"That sounds a lot like disapproval. Coming from a lawyer, being scolded for trying to make money really hurts."

She seemed intent on skewing his meaning, so he gave up attempting to explain. "Then I was out of line. Forget I said anything."

"I'm not here on vacation," she reminded him curtly as she stared out to sea. "This is my job."

And he'd do well to remember that, Cooper cautioned himself. Bree didn't belong here any more than Felicia had, and when her assignment was over, she'd be leaving. Until then his role was to play tour guide. He'd show her enough of Holiday Harbor that she'd have solid research to write a killer article convincing people to trek up the coast and visit.

Last night's cozy dinner had clearly been a fluke. As he rounded the last curve coming into Sandy Cove, he decided it was better that way.

"This is it," he announced. "Sandy Cove."

He'd braced himself, but his heart still fell at the sight of the deserted town. He drove slowly along the broken pavement, which had heaved up in large sections with the winter freeze. The houses where people had held out the longest looked fine, but other buildings hadn't fared so well in the punishing Atlantic weather. Broken glass littered what was left of the sidewalks, and shutters lay around haphazardly, as if they'd been thrown there and left to rot.

For Cooper the worst thing of all was the silence.

With no fishing boats tossing aside their scraps, even the gulls didn't come here anymore. Having grown up with their cries ringing in his ears, Cooper missed the sound. It made the place feel even more desolate than it looked.

Bree stepped down from her seat and looked around. "This is kind of creepy, isn't it? Like someone might still be here and they're watching you, waiting for you to leave."

Cooper chuckled. "Are you sure you don't write fiction on the side? You have a really good imagination."

The glare she leveled at him could have frozen the bay over in no time. "I'm a reporter. Just the facts, man."

He wondered why she was so insistent on that, then figured it was none of his business. He smiled to soothe that flash-fire temper of hers. "Got it."

"Now be quiet and let me poke around a little."

Leaning back against the front fender, he motioned for her to explore to her heart's content. "Just make sure you watch your step. Some of these buildings aren't safe."

Eyeing the decaying village with a sad expression, she asked, "What happened?"

"The fishing got bad, and then they closed the processing plant and cannery outside of town. With less jobs to be had, folks couldn't make a living here any-more, so they left."

She turned those dark, intelligent eyes on him. "You're afraid closing the dock in Holiday Harbor is the beginning of the end."

Determined to keep the town's spirits up, Cooper hadn't confided that fear to anyone outside his family. But since she'd gone there on her own, he said, "Yes, I am. I want you to help me keep this—" he nodded toward the empty street "—from happening to my home."

Understanding softened her expression, and she gave him a slight smile. "I'll do my best."

"I know."

As she strolled away from him, Cooper was surprised to discover that his vote of confidence was more than a pep talk for her benefit. Even though she hadn't set foot in Holiday Harbor until yesterday, he honestly believed she'd use her considerable talents to paint a vivid picture of his quaint but quirky hometown.

And really, he reminded himself while he thumbed through the messages on his phone, that was all he needed from her.

Wandering through the uninhabited town, Bree couldn't help imagining what it must have been like before. With people strolling along the sidewalks, and cars parked in the diagonally painted slots that made the most of the limited space. Snapping frame after frame with her camera, she began to understand why Cooper was so worried about Holiday Harbor.

Sandy Cove looked just like it.

Well, it had once, she amended with a frown. Now it stood as a solemn warning to other villages nearby not to rest on their laurels, but watch for signs of decay. Once it started, it was hard to stop.

Sweeping her viewfinder along the shoreline, she was amazed to see a figure sitting on one of the cockeyed docks. She pulled her head back and squinted into the sun, but she couldn't make out any details.

"What's that?" she asked. When Cooper looked her way, she pointed. "Someone's down there."

"Stay here and I'll check it out." He moved toward the concrete steps leading to the wharf, and she went to join him. Stopping dead, he glared at her. "I mean it, Bree. Stay here."

"Oh, come on," she wheedled, glancing down again. "He's not even moving. How dangerous can he be?"

"I'll go find out. In the meantime, wait up here."

His stern tone warned her not to argue any more, and she decided to let him have this one. She was the outsider, after all, and he knew the people around here better than she did. "Fine. But if he moves even an inch, I'm coming down there with a tire iron."

"It's good to know you've got my back."

Grinning reassurance, Cooper continued down the steps. Bree kept a close eye on the mysterious figure, then remembered she had a decent zoom lens on her camera. She lifted it and focused in, astounded by what she saw. "Uh, Cooper, I think that's a bear."

"Nah." He waved off her concern. "Looks like a Newfie."

"A what?"

Turning, he explained, "Newfoundland. They're big water dogs, with webbed feet. Great swimmers, so lots of crews have one on board to help out if someone goes into the water. He's probably just lost and looking for a way home. Do me a favor and get the little bag that's hanging behind the driver's seat. I've got some dog treats in there."

"You carry them around with you?"

"My mother's dog, Mitzy, won't let me near the house unless I bribe her first."

"Doberman?"

"Pomeranian," he corrected with a laugh. "She's cute but mean as a snake."

Unlike other lawyers she'd known, this guy slipped into the easygoing speech of regular people pretty easily. It made her wonder about the sketchy background he'd given her and how he'd come to be the way he was. Which had nothing to do with her article, of course, but it was still intriguing.

After she handed him the bag, he carefully descended the crumbling steps.

"Hey there, boy," he called out softly as he approached. "What's up?"

The dog cast a pitiful look over his shaggy shoulder, then resumed staring out at the water. Bree got the distinct impression he was waiting for someone.

Someone who wasn't coming back.

Rare tears stung her eyes, and she blinked them away as she carefully picked her way down the embankment. It was so sweet—and so sad—to see a loyal pet sitting there, gazing wistfully out to sea for a boat that wouldn't return for him. He was probably used to being out on the water with his owner, begging for scraps from the crews' lunches, enjoying his existence as their mascot.

Now he was alone, wishing his life could be the way it was back then. Sadly, Bree knew exactly how he felt.

As she got closer, she heard Cooper's low voice, speaking in a comforting tone.

"I know, boy," he commiserated, ruffling a hand through the Newfie's matted fur. "You miss 'em, don't you?"

The whimper he got in reply was startling coming from such a huge animal. His brow furrowed with canine worry, he thumped his tail on the dock and looked from Cooper to the empty bay with a hopeful expression.

The dog was filthy, but Cooper hugged him anyway. "They're not coming back, buddy. I'm sorry."

A lump of emotion blocked Bree's throat, and she swallowed hard to keep her emotions in check. This was by no means the most tragic thing she'd ever seen, but the utter loneliness of it made her heart twist with sympathy she seldom allowed herself to feel. Objectivity was the best tool a journalist had, her father always told her. It enabled them to clearly depict an event without allowing irrational feelings to cloud their account.

But right now every nerve in Bree's body felt like it was on alert, achingly aware that this forgotten pet was just the tip of the iceberg of what was happening to the traditional fishing villages in northern Maine.

"He's got a collar." Cooper's voice pulled her back from the edge, and she saw him dig it out for a better look. "A nice one, too. Leather, with a brass tag that says Sammy." Ruffling the dog's fur, he added a sad smile. "Someone really loved you, didn't they, Sammy?"

The Newfie thumped his tail, then added a quick slurp on the cheek for his new friend Cooper.

"He loved them, too," she observed angrily. "How could they just leave him behind?"

"The last family moved out a long time ago," Cooper soothed her while he fished out a treat for the dog. "My guess is they gave him to someone nearby and he ran away."

"And came back here to wait for his owner."

Cooper sighed. "Yeah. Pretty sad, huh?"

"Heartbreaking," she agreed with real feeling. "What're you gonna do with him?"

"Try to find out who he's living with now."

"And if you can't?"

Grinning, he shrugged. "I've always wanted a dog."

Sammy perked up at that comment, and as he barked his approval, Bree couldn't help laughing. "Sounds like you've got a new roomie."

"We'll see," Cooper hedged, but she could see he was already warming up to the idea of adopting the huge dog.

She finally remembered the camera in her hand and began snapping pictures of them together. Later she'd flip through and choose the best one or two to go with the article that was already writing itself in her head. A cute guy who was kind to animals? She was habitually jaded, and even she was impressed. *Kaleidoscope*'s female readers would go bonkers over this sweet, touching story.

When Cooper was out of treats, he stood and dusted the crumbs off his hands. The dog glanced from him to the water and back, whining uncertainly.

"I'm not gonna force you," Cooper told him as if he were a human who could respond. "But you can come with me if you want."

"Are you nuts?" Bree protested in fury. "You can't just leave him here."

"This guy probably weighs close to two hundred pounds. It's not like I can carry him to the car."

"But if he stays here, he'll starve to death."

"He's smarter than that." Breaking contact with her, he looked down at his new friend. "Aren't you, Sammy?"

The Newfie barked agreement, and Bree sighed in frustration. Here she stood, in an abandoned town on the edge of nowhere, outnumbered by a loony lawyer and a mutt. What on earth had happened to her nice, orderly life?

Cooper waited a few more seconds, then turned and started back up the dock. After a last longing look out to sea, the dog followed him like a puppy. A really big, really dirty puppy.

Climbing the steps like he'd done it a million times, he trotted over and sat politely in front of Bree.

"Oh, you've got to be kidding me," she grumbled, shaking her head. "Sorry, dude, but you're a mess."

Unfazed, he barked and lolled his huge tongue out, making dust devils on the ground with his tail. He was huge and filthy—and completely irresistible. Laughing, she stowed her camera and reached out to pat his head. "Good boy."

Delighted, he barked again and wriggled in place as if he was dying to jump up and hug her. Someone had trained him well, she thought with admiration. A beast like this could hurt someone without even trying.

Giving in, she set her bag on the ground a couple of feet away and held out her arms. "Gimme your best shot."

With a delighted yip, he rose up and circled his massive paws around her waist. At that height he easily planted a wet kiss on her cheek, and she couldn't keep herself from returning the friendly gesture.

They had something in common, she mused as she

hugged her unexpected new friend. Circumstances had left them on their own to fend for themselves, and they were doing the best they could.

Chapter Five

"Okay, Sammy boy," Cooper commented when he pulled into the Holiday Harbor Animal Clinic. "This is our first stop. Think you can behave yourself?"

From the backseat, he heard *thump-thump-thump* and took that for a positive response. As he swung out of his seat, Sammy dropped down neatly beside him and sat, obviously looking for instructions. This was one smart dog, Cooper thought while he waited for Bree to join them. Someone had done a remarkable training job. He hated to consider how tough it had been for the family to leave their beloved Newfie behind.

"Hey, Cooper," the receptionist greeted him. When Sammy woofed and sat down in front of the counter, her brown eyes widened in surprise. "Whoa. Who's your enormous friend?"

"Collar says Sammy," he replied, handing it over. "We found him wandering around Sandy Cove. I'm hoping he's got one of those ID chips so we can figure out where he belongs."

"We'll give it a shot." She offered her hand to Bree.

"You must be that Richmond reporter. I'm Lucy Wilson. Welcome to Holiday Harbor."

"Nice to meet you. Bree Farrell."

Lucy turned her attention back to Sammy. "So what are we doing with this cutie pie?"

Since the dog couldn't really answer, Cooper assumed her question was directed at him. "A bath first off, then find the owner."

"And if we can't?"

When he didn't answer right away, Bree snorted, "Oh, come on! You're already half in love with this walking carpet." To Lucy, she added, "He ran away from wherever he's been, and if we take him back there, he'll just keep running off. He'd do better with Cooper."

"I agree," Lucy told her. "Our mayor's got a real soft spot for dogs, you know."

"Yeah, I noticed." Grinning, Bree gave him a little wave. "You've got that meeting at your office, so I'll wait here for Sammy and we'll catch up with you later."

"There's no way you can handle him on your own," Cooper argued. Clearly insulted, Sammy woofed again, cuddling up to Bree as if she was his favorite person ever.

"Looks like you're outvoted, Cooper," Lucy teased, lifting the hinged counter to come around front.

"Traitor." Cooper's scolding got him a thigh bump that almost knocked him off his feet. Laughing, he shook his head. "Fine. Just add it all up and send me the bill."

As he turned to go, the dog began whining. He glanced back to find Bree coaxing Sammy toward the back, murmuring reassurance as they went. The Newfie shot a hesitant look over his shoulder, and Cooper stopped in his tracks. Sadly, he knew how it felt to be cast aside by someone you trusted.

Human or animal, the more intelligent someone was, the more sensitive they were to what went on around them. Clearly this dog recognized that he'd been taken from his home and wanted nothing more than to return. Since that wasn't possible, he seemed to have latched on to the first person to show him some understanding.

Cooper recalled feeling that way in New York, adrift in a sea of strangers, searching for something— anything—familiar. Once the novelty of the Big Apple had worn off, he'd missed his hometown. He'd longed for the easier pace, chatting with people on the street rather than pushing past them because he was in a hurry to get where he was supposed to be. He'd tried to fill those emotional holes with Felicia, and for a while she'd been exactly what he'd needed.

Until the day he'd realized that he was living someone else's life.

Oh, yeah, he thought while he stared back at the stray Newfie, he knew how it felt to be completely lost. Although Bree was here, Cooper felt a strange connection to the loyal dog, and he simply couldn't leave Sammy and walk out the door.

Turning back, he smiled and ruffled those muddy ears. "You know, I can talk to my clients while I wait. I'll be here when you're done, boy."

Sammy yipped, jumping up to plant a sloppy kiss on Cooper's cheek. Then, happy as a clam, he obediently trotted away with Lucy.

Cooper sat down on a nearby bench and took out his phone. While he scrolled through for the right number, Bree dropped into a chair shaped like an overturned tortoise shell, and he could feel those penetrating eyes on him. Without looking up, he asked, "What?"

"That's the sweetest thing I've ever seen in my life." He glanced over to find her beaming at him. "You, Mayor Landry, are a very nice man."

"You sound surprised."

"I am."

He'd gotten accustomed to her firm way of speaking, so the softness in her tone caught him off guard. She was a full arm's length away, but the warmth in her eyes reached the vulnerable part of him that had shut down when he'd finally accepted that Felicia loved her career more than him. He couldn't fathom how Bree had connected to it so quickly, but he couldn't deny she'd found her way there.

Since this was dangerous territory for him, he switched topics. "So why don't you tell me what you're planning to write about Sammy?"

"How did you know?"

He laughed. "I can almost see the wheels spinning in that quick mind of yours. It's a great story, right? Loyal dog waiting on a deserted dock for his owner?"

"Readers will eat it up with a spoon and beg for more," she confirmed. "But people's eyes usually glaze over when I talk about my writing with them. Are you sure you want the details?"

In answer, Cooper spread his arms across the back of the bench and got comfortable. While she described her evolving article, he found himself experiencing it all over again. Only this time he saw Sammy and himself from her perspective, which was a real eye opener. For some insane reason he was pleased to discover the jaded reporter was guarding a soft heart behind her flinty exterior.

As he got lost in the story she was telling, Cooper got the sinking feeling that it wouldn't take much for this remarkable woman to get under his skin. And this time, reminding himself she was leaving soon had no impact whatsoever.

It took two handlers more than two hours to spiff up the runaway Newfie. The vet confirmed that Sammy was neutered and updated his shots, just to be safe. He also found a chip and agreed to contact the owners, but warned Cooper not to get his hopes up.

"Based on Lucy's description of him when he got here," the man said kindly, "he's been on his own awhile. His former owners might have put the chip in, and that means it won't help us now."

Bree couldn't help feeling sorry for the dog, sitting so politely in the middle of the lobby. Freshly washed and groomed, he was an impressive sight. His fur appeared even darker now, and powerful muscles rippled under his skin when he moved. She simply couldn't believe no one wanted such a wonderful animal, and it made her unspeakably sad.

Never one for brooding, she couldn't miss the fact that Sammy's situation mirrored her own: so much to offer, but desperately searching for a place to call home. While it had national distribution, the fully digital *Kaleidoscope* wasn't anywhere near her first choice. She was accustomed to a massive audience, with readers all over the world, but for the time being Nick's fledgling magazine was all she had. And right now, she and Cooper were all Sammy had.

Crazy as it would have seemed to her only yesterday, she was head over heels in love with this dog. Since that emotion would get her absolutely nowhere, she pushed it aside and concentrated on choosing a sturdy leather leash that matched his collar. Not that she had any delusions about walking this beast, she grinned to herself. But Holiday Harbor's mayor couldn't exactly flaunt his own leash laws, could he?

When she glimpsed the bill, she gulped and braced herself for some kind of fit. She was pleasantly surprised when Cooper calmly handed over his credit card and smiled down at the dog. "I guess you're worth it."

Sammy wagged his tail in agreement, and they both laughed.

In town the sidewalks were full of afternoon traffic, and people stopped them every few yards or so to ask about their furry companion. Cooper was endlessly patient with them, even though he'd told Bree he had a call scheduled in a few minutes. She was accustomed to people zooming through their days, barely acknowledging anything outside their tunnel view. Cooper's laid-back way of dealing with everyone—human and animal alike—impressed her beyond words.

When they finally arrived at the law office next to Julia's shop, the neighboring door opened and Julia stepped out. No longer dressed for rehab work, she wore a silk tank and pale blue capris with a pair of dainty ballet-style shoes. Her china-blue eyes warmed when she saw the young lawyer.

"Hello, Cooper. Bree, it's nice to see you again."

Soft and faintly accented, Julia's cultured voice and classy appearance made Bree feel downright grungy in her rumpled traveling khakis and T-shirt. If the woman wasn't so nice, it would take no effort at all to hate her. "Nice to see you, too."

"I haven't talked to you since you got back from Martha's Vineyard," Cooper said. "How are your parents?"

She consulted a watch that probably cost more than Bree's last car. "On their way to Stuttgart for some symposium. They'll be gone the next few months, so I wanted to spend some time with them before they left." Bree recalled events like that well. Too well, actually. They'd grab a day or two as a family before Dad jetted off to some foreign country for who knew how long. She'd considered it fun until she got old enough to realize his long absences were breaking her mother's heart.

"On my way to the bank, then," Julia said. "You two enjoy your day."

The woman even walked with a lilt, Bree grumbled silently. She'd give anything to be a tenth as polished as Julia Stanton.

"Don't let her get to you," Cooper murmured. "She makes all us mortal folks look like crumbs."

Astonished that he'd guessed her general train of thought, Bree spun to face him. "How on earth did you know what I was thinking?"

He flashed her a grin that had probably melted its share of female hearts. "Bree, you're many things, but coy isn't one of them."

Responding to the teasing in his voice, she batted her eyelashes and fanned herself with her hand. "Why, counselor," she simpered in her best imitation of a Georgia peach, "you surely know how to flatter a girl."

Laughing, he opened the ornate antique door etched with Judge George Landry in bold lettering. Before going in, he considered Sammy with a thoughtful expression. "Can you behave yourself?"

In reply their furry companion sat and wagged his tail in a you-can-count-on-me way. Hoping to help him out, Bree crouched and put an arm around him. "Of course he can. He sat still for all that poking and prodding at the vet's, and he didn't whimper even once when they gave him those nasty shots. You're such a good boy," she added, flopping his ears around the way he seemed to enjoy.

"Oh, I know all that." Chuckling, Cooper pulled the door open. "It's Mrs. Andrews you have to convince. She's a cat person."

As they entered the lobby, Bree was taken aback by what she saw. Done in old-world mahogany and leather, the place smelled like leather and books. Tons of them, arranged on recessed bookshelves that were probably made from the same trees as the wainscoting framing the entire space. Large Oriental rugs softened oak floors darkened by age, and the exquisite but heavy furniture was straight out of some millionaire's mansion.

Ponderous was the word, she decided, and it didn't suit Cooper at all. Yale and NYC aside, he struck her as more rugged than refined, and hard as she tried, she couldn't picture him working here.

When she gave him a questioning look, he shrugged. "Granddad's taste, not mine."

"And you're okay with that?"

"Sure. He started the firm and worked here after he retired from the bench, so it's my way of making sure he stays part of it."

In those heartfelt words she heard the love and respect he had for his grandfather. The way he and other folks in town talked about him, the judge sounded like a real character. She wished she could have met him.

Before Bree could say anything more, they were joined by a white-haired lady wearing a tailored navy skirt suit and what Bree would describe as schoolmarm disapproval on her face. She didn't say a thing, but Cooper laughed. "Heard we were coming, huh?"

"Ten minutes ago." She eyed Sammy over her rimless half-moon glasses. "What is this?"

As Cooper relayed the Newfie's sad story, her expression warmed considerably. "You couldn't exactly leave the poor thing in Sandy Cove, could you?"

"No, ma'am."

After a few more seconds she relented. "All right, but if he makes a mess, I'm not cleaning it up."

"Yes, ma'am. Any messages for me?"

She handed over a few pink message slips. "A courier service delivered a package from Hartford about half an hour ago. It's on your desk."

"I'm not expecting anything. What is it?"

She straightened with a practiced grace that brought to mind a golden-age screen star. "Since it's addressed to you, I wouldn't know. I don't open your mail, Cooper."

"Not even to peek?" Bree asked.

"Certainly not," she answered in a precise, frosty manner. "Confidentiality is the cornerstone of a lawyer's relationship with his clients. I would never do anything to endanger that."

"Of course not," Cooper said smoothly. "Bree was only kidding."

Taking the hint, Bree jumped in. "I have a weird sense of humor, Mrs. Andrews. Please forgive me if I offended you."

"Forgiven, dear." The tone wasn't exactly warm, but it was no longer glacial, either. Bree let out a sigh of relief when the woman turned back to her boss. "Dale Hawkins just called to say he'll be in around four to sign those estate papers. Judging by the static on his phone, he's out at Shadow Lake."

"Tracking Big Wally, no doubt."

"Oh, that fish," she scoffed, dismissing it with a wave of a slender hand accented by antique rings.

"Who's Big Wally?" Bree asked.

"The stuff of legend," Cooper explained while he flipped through his messages. "Folks who've seen him say he's a ten-foot trout that can snap any fishing line ever made."

"Folks who've seen him," Mrs. Andrews chimed in while she filled two china teacups with coffee, "are highly unreliable."

"That doesn't mean they're wrong."

Setting the cups on saucers, she added them to a gleaming silver tray that held a fancy sugar bowl and real cream in a little pitcher. "I'll believe it the day someone brings him in. Cream and sugar, Miss Farrell?"

Bree hadn't introduced herself, but she'd gotten accustomed to people knowing all about her before they laid eyes on her. Smiling, she said, "Actually it's Bree, and coffee that smells this good is fine straight out of the tap."

Mrs. Andrews's expertly made-up face crinkled with a smile that showed plenty of laugh lines. Stern as she appeared on first glance, this woman clearly enjoyed her life enough to show the marks. An interesting detail and Bree mentally tagged it for later.

"How nice of you to say. If you need a place to work, you're welcome to use my side table."

"Thanks, but this is all I have." When she pulled her tablet out of her messenger bag, Bree was thrilled to see it was receiving a strong signal. She also had a dozen emails, which was a wonderful change from the leper status she'd been suffering through the past few months.

"Looks good?" Cooper asked as he led the way through to a hallway that ran the full width of the building.

"Excellent."

Mrs. Andrews set their coffee tray down and left the two of them in Cooper's office. Again Bree was awestruck by the surroundings. More wainscoting, but she also noticed his large Yale Law School diploma beautifully matted out in blue and silver. Looking closer, she saw he'd graduated with full honors. Oil paintings of seascapes hung along the walls, and massive shelves bracketed a wide window open to the breeze. She'd never had an office, and she couldn't recall the last building she'd worked in that had had functional windows. Of course most of them had been in places where you probably didn't want to be breathing the air, anyway.

Sammy seemed to approve, and he stretched out on the Oriental runner in front of Cooper's dark pedestal desk. Resting his chin on his paws, he gave a contented doggy sigh and closed his eyes.

When Cooper picked up the phone, Bree grabbed her coffee and headed for the door.

"Where are you going?" he asked.

"I'll go out front to give you some privacy. I mean, like Mrs. Andrews said, this is confidential stuff."

"Sometimes, but not now." He motioned her to a long

leather sofa that spanned the wall between the windows. "Make yourself at home," he added as he ripped open the mystery package.

She was unaccustomed to people making such an effort to help her feel at ease. Usually they were testing her, or competing with her. Or worse. She had to admit, his approach was a refreshing change of pace. "Okay. Thanks."

"No problem. Hello, Jeremy, this is Cooper Landry. I just heard from the estate that owns the property you're interested in out near Beaver Woods, and I've got good news for you."

After that the conversation devolved into real estate speak, which Bree easily tuned out. Her tablet seemed horribly out of place in the old-fashioned room, but she put that out of her mind and clicked the email icon.

As she reconnected with the world, a string of messages from Nick popped up in her in-box, and she smiled at the subject lines.

Howz it goin?

Still in HH?

Where's my intro?

She opened the latest one, sent earlier this morning, and typed, In HH, going fine, story on its way.

Glancing across the room, she saw Cooper at his own keyboard but refrained from looking at the monitor to see what he was doing. Her eyes drifted down to the sleeping dog, and she thought back over their very eventful day. Words began arranging themselves in her head, and she started typing before they vanished.

She wrote a vivid description of Holiday Harbor, to make people want to pack up the kids and the car and head to northern Maine. After a quick proofread, she emailed it to him before she had a chance to think better of it. Less than five minutes later her email alert chimed with his reply: Perfect.

She stared at it for a long time, hardly daring to trust what she'd seen. But it didn't change, and she relaxed. Absorbing what it meant, she savored the praise from the man she hoped would become her new editor.

Maybe, she thought with a smile, this wacky assignment would prove to be the fresh start she needed.

Chapter Six

Bree shook her head when Cooper and his passenger pulled in at the lighthouse on Sunday morning. "Let me guess. He wouldn't let you leave."

Sammy was stretched out across the entire backseat of the open-air car. Hearing her voice, he whacked his tail and panted his version of "hello."

"I felt bad leaving him inside, and I couldn't trust him to stick around a strange place till I got back."

"You're such a softie." She reached over the side to give Sammy a little love, then swung into her seat and fastened her seat belt.

"Do me a favor and keep it under your hat."

"I've got news for you, counselor. Everyone already knows."

She made that sound like a good thing, and he smiled as he drove back up the lane. "I've got some news I think you're gonna like. The vet got hold of Sammy's owners, and they came to my place last night."

Was it his imagination, or did she frown before asking, "Oh, yeah? What did they say?"

"They were friends of his original owners, who

moved to Cleveland and didn't feel right confining him to an apartment. Anyway, this family's had him for more than a year, and he's run away six times. They've tried a kennel with a run, invisible fence, everything but tying him up while they're gone."

"Which would be mean," she insisted sternly.

She really had a thing for this dog, Cooper realized. Maybe the icy heart image she projected so well was her way of ensuring she didn't get hurt. The fact that she'd mentioned previous mistakes but didn't elaborate spoke volumes about just how hard a fall she'd taken.

He could relate to that.

"Anyway," he continued, "they wanted to meet me, to make sure I'll take good care of him. I passed muster, so Sammy's mine."

The Newfie barked, and she laughed. "I think he's psyched about that."

Feeling pretty chipper himself, Cooper grinned. "So am I."

After a couple of miles the chronic impatience he'd noticed in Bree yesterday finally bubbled to the surface. "There are three churches right in town. Where are we going?"

"The Captains' Chapel. It was built in 1852, and my family's been going there ever since."

"You're kidding."

"Nope."

Angling to face him, she pressed. "Why? What makes it so special?"

"You'll see."

"The last time you said that, we ended up with him."

She pointed a thumb back at Sammy, and Cooper wondered if she realized she'd said "we" instead of "you." He wasn't sure what that meant, but he liked the sound of it. Probably more than he should have. "Surprises can be good, Bree."

"Not in my world."

Her bitter response sounded like an opening, and he suspected she'd confide in him if he nudged her a little. "Tell me about Boston."

She groaned, but faced him directly when she answered. "The paper I was working for had a team doing a series on senators running for reelection. One day I found out the incumbent was in town. Secretly."

"Sounds intriguing."

"It was." She sighed. "Anyway, I managed to find out where he was headed and got there first. It was a strip club, and I saw him pull some money out of his wallet for a young blonde dancer. Then he gave her a long hug and walked her out to his car. When they drove off together, you can imagine what I thought."

Cooper personally knew the senator she was talking about, a highly respected man who'd devoted his life to public service. "I don't have to imagine. I read about it on some blog before the facts were clear. Half the people in the country did."

If he'd known Bree had been responsible for breaking the false story, he never would have agreed when Nick suggested she cover Holiday Harbor. No doubt his old buddy had suspected as much, which was why he'd neglected to mention it.

"I was so wrong," she confided in a voice filled with regret. "She was his granddaughter, and he'd snuck away from a campaign appearance to beg her to come home. The money he gave her was to pay off her landlord, and he took her with him so she wouldn't run away again.

He was there to rescue her, and I made him look like a perverted old man."

Cooper wasn't exactly thrilled with her right now, and he didn't bother hiding his opinion. "You're fortunate he didn't sue you."

"His lawyer wanted him to, but the senator came to see me first. That's how I finally learned the truth, and I was mortified. When I apologized, he stared down at me as if he was trying to decide how to punish a child. Then he said he believed everyone deserves a second chance and promised not to take me to court. I thought he was nuts."

"It's called forgiveness," Cooper informed her coolly. "And not many would've done what he did. Your second chance came straight out of the Bible. You can look it up."

She gave him a long look, then continued. "My boss wasn't as generous, and since my track record isn't that great, he took advantage of a golden opportunity to get rid of me. Mad as I was, I couldn't really blame him. I screwed up one time too many, and paid the price." Sitting back, she folded her hands in her lap and stared blankly out the windshield. "So that's my shameful story, Mr. Mayor. Not very pretty."

What an understatement, he thought grimly, fearing her tendency to jump to conclusions would negatively affect her portrayal of his hometown. Not for the first time, he considered telling her to forget about the article and go back to Richmond.

Then again, she seemed honestly sorry for what she'd done. Oddly enough it was her quick connection with Reggie and Sammy that ended his internal debate. Anyone who bonded with animals that way couldn't be all bad.

Since he shared the senator's philosophy on second chances, he opted to follow the man's gracious example. "Maybe not, but Nick's convinced you've learned your lesson. He and I might not always see eye to eye, but he's usually bang-on when it comes to people. I'll trust his judgment on this one."

"Are you serious?"

He chuckled. "Not always, but this time, yes."

Cooper didn't say anything more, but he could almost hear the wheels spinning in her head while she tried to decide if he truly meant what he'd said. When they drove around a curve and headed toward the water's edge, he glanced over to gauge her reaction.

Her wide-open mouth was all the approval he could have asked for.

Slightly up off the water the pale gray chapel blended seamlessly with the massive chunk of granite it was built on. Beyond it stretched miles of open ocean, the bluish-green water sparkling like jewels as the waves ebbed and flowed. Not a single cloud marred the scene, allowing full sunshine to light the picture-perfect view.

"It's breathtaking," she murmured, reaching for her camera. "Can we stop here a minute?"

Mentally patting himself on the back, Cooper pulled over. "Sure. Take your time."

These were the images he wanted people to see. Coupled with Bree's vivid words, they'd showcase all that Holiday Harbor had to offer. Unspoiled and wild, it was the only place he'd ever been that could make him forget everything but how incredibly beautiful God's handiwork was.

When she was finished snapping pictures, he parked in the small gravel lot and reached back to clip the leash on Sammy's collar. The Newfie gave him an "are you kidding me?" look, and Cooper wagged a finger at him. "I know you're not going anywhere, but we've got rules around here. Since you're with me, they'll let you in, but we have to make it look good."

The dog sighed, but jumped down and patiently plodded alongside Cooper. Bree, not so much. .

"This is awesome!" Rushing toward the door, she paused beside the old ship's bell that hung in the place of honor. The antique brass was kept at a mirror polish, and she leaned in to read the inscription. Sarah Anne. 1850. Twenty-nine souls surrendered to God.

"Jeremiah Landry's ship," Cooper explained. "A bad storm threw her onto the rocks, and he went down with her. His pregnant wife, Sarah, was waiting at the pier for him and saw the whole thing. The following year she convinced the town to build the lighthouse."

Bree got a few shots of the chapel, and several close-ups of the bell. Lowering her camera, she gave him a thoughtful look. "It's unusual for a family to be so rooted in one place these days. Nice, though," she added quickly.

After enduring her not-so-subtle digs at his hometown, he found her kinder attitude much easier to take. "Yeah, I like it. Should we head inside?"

She eyed the open double doors as if she expected them to swallow her whole. Cooper had met plenty of folks who were uncomfortable with going to church. Seemed like she was one of them, but he was counting on her innate curiosity to help her overcome that. He wasn't disappointed.

"Sure."

The clipped response sounded uncertain, but he ignored that and strolled confidently inside. Just in case Sammy got restless, Cooper chose a seat in the back. Now that he thought about it, Bree would do better here, too. It was such a pleasant morning, the pastor would leave the doors open to let in the breeze. With the sunshine and blue sky just a glance away, she'd probably feel more at ease near the edge of the congregation.

Several people stopped to wish them a good morning and meet the already notorious Sammy, who obligingly allowed them to pet him and say what a handsome dog he was. If Cooper didn't know better, he'd think the Newfie was playing the crowd.

"What a ham," Bree muttered while she flicked through pictures on her camera.

"That reminds me, the vet only had one bag of food for him. I need to pick up some more."

"Lots more."

They traded a smile, and he caught that rare sparkle in her eyes. How many men other than him had seen it? During dinner the other night, she'd seemed content with her single status. Still it was hard to believe she'd never bent the rules for someone, and he wondered what it would take for her to put them aside.

Almost immediately he chided himself for going there. He'd had more than his fill of driven career women, no matter how good a heart they were hiding beneath all that ambition.

The pastor moved through the chapel, greeting people here and there with a handshake and a friendly smile. He was a lot younger than she'd anticipated, probably only a few years older than Cooper. When his eyes landed on her, Bree's impulse was to duck behind Cooper and remain as invisible as possible. *Everyone knows you're in town,* she reminded herself sternly. *Buck up and act like an adult.*

Sitting up a little straighter, she gave the man what she hoped came across as a pleasant nod. His dark eyes lit up, and he made a beeline for the back of the church. Her heart racing with panic, she searched her mind for something to say when he got there.

To her great relief he brushed past her and knelt on the floor to pet the sprawling Newfie's head. "Hello there, big fella. I've been hearing a lot about you."

"No doubt." Cooper grinned over at him. "Pastor Allen, this is Sammy."

The minister held out his hand, and the dog shook it as if it was the most natural thing in the world for him to do. "Pleased to meet you, Sammy." He stood and focused on Bree. "And you, Miss Farrell. I'm thrilled to see you this morning."

"Thank you." Not to be outdone by a dog, she offered her hand. "You have a beautiful church."

"We think so. I'm sure Cooper told you some of its history, but if you have any questions, just let me know."

"She's *my* guest," Mavis interrupted from behind him. "Any questions she's got about this town, I'll be answering them."

Inserting herself between the two of them, she plunked herself down on the bench next to Bree and opened a hymnal. Squinting at the board listing today's songs, she licked her fingertip and flipped through the yellowed pages to the opening hymn.

"I don't want to start a fight or anything," Bree

hedged, glancing at Cooper for backup. Suddenly fascinated by the ceiling fan spinning overhead, he was no help at all.

"You're not," the pastor assured her with a generous smile. "Mavis is our town historian. If you'll excuse me, I see some more new faces today."

After he'd gone, Bree leaned in and whispered to Mavis, "That wasn't very nice. He was only trying to help."

"You've got all the help you need, honey."

The older woman cast a sidelong look at Cooper, then eyed Bree with a "you know what I mean" kind of expression. Unfortunately Bree had no clue what she was supposed to understand. Then it hit her, and she laughed quietly. "Pastor Allen's single, isn't he?"

Mavis nodded. "He's nice enough, but he's not right for you."

"I'm leaving Tuesday morning," Bree pointed out. "What could possibly happen between now and then?"

Another look at Cooper, who'd finally decided to pay attention to their odd little exchange.

"Mavis," he said in a firm but gentle tone, "Bree has a life in Richmond to get back to."

The logical explanation tripped right off his tongue, and normally Bree would have agreed without even thinking about it. But these days it wasn't actually true, and she almost said so. Then she thought again and decided against it. Nothing was pulling her back to Richmond, but she didn't want anyone getting the idea that spending extra time in Holiday Harbor was on her list of things to do.

Bree had accepted Cooper's invitation to attend services as a way to study another element of daily life in the close-knit community. She hadn't been to church since her mother used to drag her there as a child, so she was sorely out of practice. She carefully followed Cooper's lead, and he thoughtfully pointed out the readings and hymns so she could keep up. When the pastor began a sermon on fortitude, she forced herself to stare at the pulpit and listen.

Bree hated being preached to, and she'd endured so much of it lately she'd become adept at tuning it out. But Pastor Allen's sermon was more like a story, focused on a fisherman lost in a hurricane. Praying to God for guidance, he navigated his boat through the storm and his faith in the Almighty was rewarded with a safe harbor. There, the crew were able to make repairs and restock their food for the long journey home.

The allegory struck her like poetry, and she followed along with his portrayal of God guiding people through trying times. The only condition: they had to be humble enough to get down on their knees and ask for His help.

Completely absorbed in the tale, Bree couldn't shake the feeling that the preacher was speaking to her. Somehow he'd recognized that she was one of those struggling people, and he was showing her the path that would lead her to what she was missing.

Shaken by the idea, she mentally pulled away and gazed out a nearby window, hoping to find something out there to reground her. They were so close to the ocean, she could hear the faint sound of crashing waves. Rolling in and receding, in an endless cycle that had gone on forever and would continue until the end of time. It made her feel tiny by comparison, until she noticed the lighthouse in the distance.

Last Chance, she mused with a frown. For the first

time she considered the possibility that it wasn't a co-incidence that she'd landed in Holiday Harbor. This assignment was her own last chance to get her career back on track. Like those ships headed for the rocks, she'd gone pretty far off course, totally unaware that she was steering herself into disaster.

Her spectacular downfall was no accident, she finally admitted. Her former colleagues and editors hadn't conspired to ruin her career out of jealousy or spite. Out of arrogance she'd done it to herself, and she'd gotten what she deserved. And now, sitting in this pretty church on a bright Sunday morning, an eerie calm came over her, like nothing she'd ever experienced before. She felt her bitterness recede a little, replaced with something she hadn't felt much lately.

Hope.

Sammy whined, and she found him eyeing her, his forehead creased with canine worry. Smiling, she reached down and ruffled the thick fur on his neck so he'd know she was okay. Thumping his tail, he licked her hand, then pressed his head into her palm in a silent plea for some more love. Which, of course, she gave him without thinking twice.

Mavis was right about animals, she thought with a little grin. They didn't try to scam you, or tell you one thing when they meant the opposite. If only more people were like that, Bree would get along with them just fine.

When the service was over, Cooper introduced her around the congregation, and she made mental notes. One man ran the marina, another the local movie theater. Two sisters—Georgia Bynes and Carolina Appleton—owned the bakery in town. In near unison they invited her to stop by Holiday Harbor Sweets tomorrow morning before the Fourth of July celebration for some fresh orange scones. For the life of her she couldn't tell them apart, but they had syrupy Southern accents and struck her as being genuinely delightful.

Dressed in their refined Sunday best, they were obviously on their good behavior now, but their less-than-subtle winks told her she'd stumbled on the town's informal news network. She couldn't wait to hear what they had to say about the contentious housing project Cooper had mentioned. She suspected these two would offer up a very different perspective than their pragmatic, even-keeled mayor.

Once she and Sammy were settled in the car, Cooper stood inside her open door. "Are you okay?"

"Sure. Why?"

"Near the end of the sermon, you were staring out at the lighthouse, and you looked—I don't know—sad."

"Pensive," she corrected, intentionally using the word he'd cautioned her about. His faint grin told her she hadn't quite managed to sound casual about it. She couldn't believe he'd been watching her so closely, or that he cared enough about a near stranger to be worried about her. Apparently he and Sammy had quite a bit in common. "I'm fine, really. Thanks for asking, though."

He studied her for a few moments, then nodded in a way that said he knew that wasn't the whole truth, but wouldn't push her for more. Bree had met very few people who respected other people's wishes so well. Just another mark in the pro column for Cooper Landry, she decided as they drove back to the lighthouse. One of these days some Holiday Harbor girl was going to land herself a real catch.

After waving goodbye to the mayor and his dog, she

declined a game of backgammon with Mavis and headed upstairs to get some work done. Small but neat, the tower room was decorated like an old ship's stateroom, right down to the iron-railed widow's walk. The door stuck, but with a good yank, it opened to allow the scent and sound of the ocean inside.

Bree cautiously tested the floor of the small balcony, making sure it was still solid. When she was satisfied, she spread her hands wide and leaned on the railing to look out at the water. There were a few boats out, and she even noticed a couple of sailboarders braving the waves. It was pretty breezy, so they were flying across the water, their colorful sails flat-out.

She heard the faint clanging of a bell somewhere over the horizon, and watched as a good-sized pleasure boat crested the waves and headed for the harbor. How many women had stood here over the centuries, watching and waiting, praying for their men to come home safely?

Praying?

Where had that come from? she wondered, shaking the errant thought from her head. The pastor's sermon must have made more of an impression on her than she'd realized. Turning, she went back inside and started drafting her article. Staring at the pages of notes she'd accumulated, she sighed. "I've got enough here for a whole book about Holiday Harbor."

A quiet scratching at her door was a much-needed distraction, and she reached over to open it for Reggie. Placing his neatly trimmed hooves on the quilt, he gave her a look that clearly said, "I want up."

She wasn't keen on having him for an assistant, but he was so cute she couldn't resist. "Okay, but don't mess with anything."

He grunted a reply, and jumped up on a chair before joining her on the bed. After she gave him a rubdown, he made himself comfortable and curled up for a nap. "Wish I could join you," she grumbled with a yawn.

Hoping for inspiration, she picked up her phone and started scrolling through the candid pictures she'd taken since arriving. Nothing sparked an idea until she got to the last one from Sandy Cove.

Framed by the waterline, it showed Cooper sitting with Sammy, his arm around the filthy dog as if comforting him while they both stared out to sea. The quality wasn't nearly what she'd get from her camera, but it really didn't matter.

While she was practical by nature, the raw emotion in that single picture actually made her heart ache. It was as if Cooper and Sammy were both waiting for someone to come back into their lives, even though they knew it was never going to happen.

Blinking back tears, Bree started typing. She poured out Sammy's story, ending with the scene that had touched her so deeply. Knowing Cooper would resent such an intrusion, she left him out but made it clear that the brave, loyal dog had found a home with someone who loved and appreciated him just the way he was.

She monkeyed with several titles before settling on a phrase from the story: "Loyal and True." Reading it centered at the top choked her up again, and since that was the reaction she wanted to evoke in her readers, she figured it was ideal.

She prepared an email to Nick, but the wireless signal didn't reach into the tower. Too lazy to go down all those stairs to the parlor, she dialed Nick's number.

"If you're gonna be late, I don't wanna hear it."

"How could I be late?" she asked sweetly. "It's only July third."

"Right. Sorry. What did you need?"

When she explained her disconnectedness, he laughed derisively. "Gotta love that place."

"It's real short," she pressed, trying to contain her excitement so he'd be surprised. "Do you have time to listen to it?"

"Shoot."

"First I want to send you a picture." She texted it to him and waited until he confirmed he'd gotten it.

"Is that Cooper hugging that mess of a dog?"

"Yes, but keep that part to yourself. Now look at the photo while I read this to you."

"Man, you're bossy all of a sudden," he grumbled. "This better be good."

It took her about two minutes to recite the entire thing. When she was finished, the line was dead silent. She'd poured her heart into this piece, and she was desperate for his opinion, but she tamped down her anxiety and let him absorb it.

"You wrote that?" he demanded. "Just now?"

"Yes."

He muttered something she didn't catch, then she heard his fingers clacking away on his keyboard. After a few seconds he said, "I've got just enough space for this tomorrow. I'll bump one of the ongoing ads and double its size on Tuesday to keep the client happy."

Bree felt her eyes double in size, too. The alterations weren't impossible, obviously, but unnecessary changes were strictly against *Kaleidoscope* policy. They cost money, and Nick hated losing money even more than he hated reporters missing their deadlines. "You want to run it tomorrow?"

"Absolutely. I'll pay you the same rate, but it's not much since the word count is so small."

"That's okay," she breathed, closing her eyes as relief washed over her. She'd taken a huge risk sharing such a personal story with him, and she really appreciated the reception he'd given it. "Thank you, Nick."

"Thank me, nothing. This is all you, Farrell. Nobody in this business ever doubted your talent, it was your attitude they had a problem with. Me, I don't care if you're not Miss Congeniality. I just want more stories like this. Got it?"

"Got it."

"One more thing before the wind blows away your cell signal. Have you got a title for the larger article yet?"

"I was thinking about 'Fireworks at Holiday Harbor.'"

"I like it." More tapping told her he'd already dropped it into the layout. "If that article is anything like this one, we'll be talking again real soon."

They both hung up, and Bree set her phone on the quilt, staring at it for a full minute while she tried to wrap her head around what had just happened. Sitting here in a creaky old lighthouse with a pig snoozing on her bed, she was on the verge of resurrecting the career she'd come within inches of losing.

Still a little dazed, she went out on the widow's walk for some fresh air. Gazing out at the ocean, she felt a sudden wave of gratitude.

Thinking back to Pastor Allen's sermon, she wondered if it was really possible that God had stripped away all the things she thought she wanted, shoving her on to a much better path than the one she'd chosen herself.

A ray of sunlight fanned out on the shore below her, and she couldn't help thinking it was meant for her.

"I can't believe you talked me into this," Bree complained from her seat in *Stargazer*'s bow. "This is way faster than I thought we'd be going."

Laughing, Cooper stepped around her and angled the main sail to catch more of the wind. "It wasn't me who talked you into running the regatta. It was him."

He nodded toward his furry navigator, who barked at them before turning his nose back into the wind. They were midpack, and Sammy kept up a steady stream of encouraging sounds. If he'd been able to speak canine, Cooper had no doubt the intelligent Newfie could direct him across the finish line in first place.

A boa constrictor wouldn't be wrapped around Bree as tightly as her life jacket was, but as they rounded the far buoy, he noticed she'd relinquished her stranglehold on the railing. A few minutes later she was comfortable enough to take out her camera and start snapping pictures of the other racers.

"Is that George and Martha Washington?" she asked as she lined up a shot.

"Sure is. Right behind them you've got Thomas Jefferson, and I think that's Paul Revere on the jet ski."

Cooper tacked across the waves to slow down a bit. When she glared back at him, he knew she'd caught on to his strategy.

"You're not even trying to win this race," she accused with narrowed eyes. "Why not?"

"I'm the mayor. Besides, I won the trophy last year, so it's someone else's turn."

Amusement sparkled in her eyes. "Let me guess. It's a big brass cup you need two people to lift."

"Actually it's a pewter goblet Jeremiah Landry used on the Sarah Anne. They found it offshore after she sank, and it was passed down through my family. They donated it as the trophy years ago, when the race first started. Back then the real prize was the first slip at the dock for the rest of the season."

"Cool." Bree took a few more pictures, then without looking up said, "All the history around here is really—"

"Odd?"

"Nice," she corrected with a smile. "It gives the town a solid feeling I don't get in very many places. Like it will always be here, no matter what."

The fondness in her tone told him they'd finally cracked through her tough exterior, and she'd fallen for the quirky charm of his hometown. Returning the smile, he said, "We've been here a long time, through blizzards and hurricanes, even a plague or two. We're too stubborn to be taken down by a bunch of spreadsheets."

While they cruised past the final marker, she laughed. "That's good to hear. But right now, you should be thinking up a good story about why you lost this race."

"I'll just tell them you distracted me with an endless stream of questions," he said with a wink. "They'll believe that."

The sassy reporter actually stuck her tongue out at him, and he glided into his assigned slip, laughing like a maniac.

Chapter Seven

When the race was over, Bree watched Cooper expertly tack into his spot and toss a mooring line to Jack. No doubt about it: the man knew his way around a boat.

A huge grin splitting his weathered features, the old fisherman chortled. "Got ya this time, boy. I been here five minutes."

"Nice run, Jack," Cooper replied, reaching over to shake his gnarled hand. "You managed that crosswind a lot better than I did."

Cocking his head, the old salt regarded him with a skeptical eye. "Don't be shoveling it on, son. We all know you dropped off and let us win. Course," he added with a wicked grin at Bree, "my first mate's Grover, not this pretty thing here. I reckon I wasn't as distracted as you."

Cooper grinned and occupied himself with coiling up one of the countless ropes that seemed to sprout up in the sailboat all on their own. As Jack sauntered off, Bree followed Cooper and Sammy up onto the dock.

"I guess you called that one," she teased.

Turning to face her, Cooper shrugged. "Folks think

what they want to, and it's pretty hard to change their minds."

"But there's nothing going on here." She motioned from herself to him and back. "I wish people wouldn't just assume otherwise."

Folding his arms, he gave her a curious look. "Why?"

"Because it's not true."

The last few stragglers passed them, laughing and joking on their way up to The Crow's Nest. For some reason, though, Cooper didn't join them. Instead he took another step toward her, pinning Bree with a very intense look totally at odds with the laid-back demeanor she'd come to expect from him.

He didn't say a word, but something she couldn't begin to define warmed his summer-sky eyes. Bree opened her mouth to say something, but her mind had gone completely to mush. There was hardly any space between them, and she could feel the sun warming his skin. For the first time she noticed the streaks of gold in his hair, and that he smelled like the ocean breeze swirling around them.

Stepping back, she said, "I'm here on assignment, and I'm leaving tomorrow. Remember?"

"I remember."

But I could stay, she almost blurted before she caught herself. Despite her best efforts, she was falling for this very appealing guy. It wasn't just his looks, although on their own they'd have been tempting enough. No, it was his agile wit and warm heart that had drawn her in and made her want to extend her visit.

Her parents' chaotic marriage and heart-wrenching divorce flooded into her mind, kicking back any thoughts of pursuing something with Cooper. This was a man for keeping, not for messing around with. And right now she had her hands full just taking care of herself.

Hoping to keep things light, she said, "I have to get back to Richmond so Nick doesn't forget about me."

An admiring male grin slowly spread across his tanned face. "Bree, I doubt there's a man alive who could ever forget about you."

No one had ever spoken to her like that, and she felt a flattered blush creeping over her cheeks. "Really?"

"Really."

Although he sounded sincere, the light in his eyes had dimmed, and he gave her something between a smile and a frown. He turned and called for Sammy, stopping here and there to greet the latecomers as he strolled up the gangway. Watching him go, it took every ounce of her resolve to keep from running after him and telling him she'd changed her mind.

"Oh, man." Bree laughed as the parade got underway. "Is that goat dressed like Uncle Sam?"

Cooper followed the direction her zoom lens was pointed and nodded. "Looks pretty good, too. He just might win the costume contest."

"Does that actually happen?"

"Last year a boat won for best-dressed." Pulling her camera away, she cocked a dubious brow, and he held up his hand. "Honest. You never know what these judges will do."

"You should've seen Mavis getting Reggie into his Teddy Roosevelt outfit after breakfast this morning. The little oinker was eating up all that attention, even posing for pictures. I think she's right—he likes pretending to be someone else."

"Yeah, he's a ham."

Giggling, she shook a scolding finger at him. "That was *so* not funny."

Cooper managed to keep a straight face, but it was tough. "What?"

"No meat jokes about Reggie. It's not nice."

Cooper laughed, and she smacked his shoulder before turning her attention back to the parade. The school band marched past, playing a medley of patriotic songs and wearing their new uniforms. Made of wool, they were meant for football season rather than summer performances, but the musicians had voted to wear them anyway, to thank the town for donating the considerable funds to purchase them. He wondered if the kids were second-guessing themselves now.

A group of Revolutionary War reenactors marched past, mostly in step with the rim shots on the antique drum. The breeze swirled through the first American flag ever flown over Holiday Harbor, lovingly preserved and brought out for special occasions. When the fife player began "Stars and Stripes Forever," everyone along the parade route cheered and waved their own flags.

"This is so cool," Bree said, snapping frame after frame. "I can't remember the last time I went to a parade."

Her comment struck him as odd, since he attended them all year long. Then again, when you didn't settle in one place for any length of time, you missed out on things other folks took for granted.

Not wanting her to overlook anything, he tapped the top of her camera with his finger. "You miss a lot staring at the screen."

"Like what?"

He pointed farther down the route where David Bird-sall and half a dozen others in period costumes were approaching on their high-wheel bikes. When she spun around to line up a shot, Cooper gave her a chiding look.

"One more, I promise. Then I'll watch." She kept her word, and after a few minutes, she patted his shoulder to get his attention. When he looked down, she gave him a grateful smile.

"You're right. This is much better." To his surprise, she hugged his arm and added, "I want to thank you for all your help the past few days. It must have been a pain entertaining me and answering so many questions, but you were really great."

"It was my pleasure. You're a lot of fun to hang out with."

"Thanks." This smile had a tinge of regret in it, and she quickly looked away. With her gaze fixed on the 4-H horseback group, she sighed. "I can't believe it, but I've really started to like this place."

She seemed so wistful, he almost suggested that she stay awhile longer. But she'd been pretty clear about how important it was for her to go, and he decided it was best not to bring it up. If she wanted to spend more time here, he'd made it plain she was welcome, not only by the town but by him personally. Much as he'd enjoy getting to know her better, he'd learned long ago that trying to change a woman's mind about anything was a waste of time and energy.

"Cooper!"

When he heard his mother calling him, he found a red, white and blue parasol bobbing through the crowd toward where he stood with Bree. Embellished with bunting and shiny fireworks streamers, the souvenir from a friend's wedding was her "going to the parade" umbrella. The fact that it was the perfect accessory for her handmade Betsy Ross outfit was just a bonus.

Sammy suddenly rose to his feet, pointing like a hunting dog toward something Cooper couldn't see yet. When he noticed what had gotten the Newfie's attention, he groaned.

"Uh-oh," he muttered when he saw Mitzy tucked under Mom's arm. "Dog alert."

"That's not a dog," Bree murmured back. "It's a dust bunny with legs."

"That's Mitzy," he explained quietly. "I got her for Mom one Christmas so she'd have some company when I was living in New York. Now that I'm back, the little brat hates me."

Eyes twinkling with humor, Bree smirked. "A rival for your mother's attention. Isn't that cute?"

"Sure, till she takes a chunk out of your ankle." As a precaution, he wrapped Sammy's sturdy leash around his hand one more time and patted the dog's head. "I know she looks like lunch, but if you try to eat her, you're toast."

The Newfie gave him the most disdainful look he'd ever gotten in his life, and Bree laughed. "I think he's telling you he wouldn't bother with anything that small."

"Let's hope so. Hey, Mom." Greeting her with a kiss on the cheek, he motioned to Bree. "I'd like you to meet Bree Farrell. Bree, this is my mother, Amelia Landry."

"Amelia Earhart Landry," she corrected him as she shook the reporter's hand. "The lady was a close friend of my grandfather's."

"Is that so?" Bree egged her on with a smile. "How did he know her?"

"Very well."

She added an unmistakable wink, and Bree's smile deepened to show some rare dimples. "I'd love to hear more about that. Will you be at Cooper's barbecue later?"

"Of course. If I'm not there, all he serves is meat and crackers. No salads, no desserts, you know how men are."

"Definitely." Bree slanted a look up at him, eyes twinkling with delight at his mother's ribbing.

Cooper did his best to appear unconcerned, but Mom was giving his new buddy The Eye. "This must be the notorious Sammy."

Taking his cue, the Newfie offered her one of his enormous paws. Clearly impressed, she gave it a gentle shake. "Good boy."

He batted his tail on the ground, and Mitzy yapped her opinion of him. The whole thing was so ridiculous, Cooper had to laugh. "I think they like each other."

Mom patted the dog's shaggy head, then looked over at Bree. "I heard you were at Sandy Cove that day, too. Exciting, wasn't it?"

"Very. He's a fabulous dog, and really smart. I think he and Cooper belong together."

To Cooper's ears, her response came across as pretty personal, and curiosity sparked in his mother's blue eyes. She didn't say anything, but he knew she'd been keeping tabs on him through the gossip mill. She must know he'd been spending a lot of time with their guest, and he could imagine her reading all kinds of things into that statement.

"Bree's article is coming right along," he said to shift

the conversation back on track. "She's going to help us put Holiday Harbor on the map."

"Actually we've already started. I did a quick piece about Sammy, and Nick put it online at midnight. We've had a hundred thousand reads already, which is unheard of for a holiday."

This was news to him, and Cooper stared in disbelief. "A hundred thousand? That's incredible."

"Wonderful," Amelia agreed, patting Bree's arm with a white glove. "Congratulations."

"Thanks. It's the lead-in to tomorrow's main story," she explained to Cooper, "which I'm hoping to email from your office in the morning. The lighthouse wireless comes and goes, and I want to make sure it gets through."

"It's done?"

"Mostly. I want to add some details about the actual Fourth celebration, but I'll finish that tonight, so it'll be ready to go first thing tomorrow."

And then, Cooper thought with a sinking heart, so would she. Shoving the thought aside, he asked, "Anyone for caramel apples?"

"No, but the smell of that popcorn is making me ravenous." Collapsing her parasol, his mother hooked it over the waistband of her apron and put her free arm around Bree's shoulders. "I'm sure Cooper's bored you to death with stories about settlers and sea captains. Come with me, and I'll fill you in on the more juicy Landry family history."

"Most of which you can't prove," Cooper reminded her as they strolled ahead of him.

Bree tossed a mischievous grin back at him, and he laughed at the picture they made. The no-nonsense reporter dressed for work, and his lovably eccentric mother who took any opportunity to play dress-up. What a pair.

For town events the Business Development Committee paid the vendors for their supplies, so everything was free for the people milling around the square. Cooper was glad to see a wide variety of food stands alternating with games and local history displays.

Mavis stood beside the lighthouse presentation, answering questions for a family he didn't recognize. Looking around, he noticed others, and he nodded to himself in satisfaction. Seeing them here reinforced his belief that what Holiday Harbor needed was publicity. Once tourists found them, the town would sell itself.

At least, that's what he kept telling himself.

When Cooper invited her to help him sail *Stargazer* back to his place later that afternoon, Bree jumped at the opportunity. The race had been so much fun, she was eager for more time on the water. As they approached his dock, she sighed. "Another gorgeous day. Do you order them up just for the tourists, Mr. Mayor?"

"Absolutely," he replied with a chuckle. "We don't allow any rain till after Labor Day."

"I've seen this side of the bay from the lighthouse, but I didn't notice any houses. Do you live up in the trees or something?"

"Kind of. I like it quiet, and I've always loved this place. It was Granddad's, and we had some great times here. He knew that, so he left it to me."

As the trees gave way to a wide clearing, she couldn't believe the view. "Wow."

"I thought you were a city girl."

"I am, but this is really pretty. Like one of those

screen savers people use to make them feel like they've gotten away from the office for a little while."

A small log house sat at the end of a weathered dock, which gave the place a rustic, lived-in look. A far cry from the family's Victorian homestead on Main Street, the waterfront cabin with its wraparound deck seemed to be much more Cooper's style.

Spotlights spaced under the eaves glowed dimly, giving the place an inviting appearance. She assumed they'd brighten as the sun went down, which was much better than coming home to a dark house.

While Cooper unlocked the front door and motioned her inside, she asked, "Aren't you going to get Sammy?"

Cooper glanced out to where the dog, who still stood in the boat, was doing a fair impression of a ship's figurehead. One happily wagging its tail. "I think if he was going to run off, he'd have done it by now. He looks like he's having fun out there, so we'll leave him be. He'll come in when he's ready."

"O-kay."

Dragging the word out in a doubtful tone, she cast a worried look over her shoulder before going inside. Just inside the door, what she saw stopped her in her tracks.

These weren't your typical lawyer's digs.

She'd known a few, and none of them would be caught dead living in a place like this. Rustic but neat as a pin, the cabin looked like a photo shoot for *Field and Stream*. The overstuffed leather furniture had that lived-in look that made you want to curl up in front of the fire and read one of the leather-bound books from the shelves built around the stone fireplace. The hefty mantel looked like it had been hacked from an old tree by hand, and the openmouthed fish hanging in the place of honor was big enough to serve a family of four.

Everything appeared to have been here forever, and like the office, she assumed Cooper had left it just the way it was out of fondness for his grandfather. Bree didn't have good memories of any one place in particular, and she felt a twinge of envy for Cooper's strong connection to his past.

Family pictures were clustered along the mantel, and she picked a young Cooper out of several. On a shelf nearby she noticed trophies for everything from soccer to debating, and one in particular made her turn and stare at him. "You were a football player?"

"Quarterback," he replied as he flipped on some lights.

"A pretty good one," she added, trying to get him to brag a little. "Most guys don't have hardware like that next to their collection of Shakespeare and Edgar Allan Poe."

"I guess not. *Tamerlane and Other Poems* is a first edition, if you're interested."

Stunned, she firmly clasped her hands together to keep them from reaching out to grab it. "You're kidding."

"Have a look."

"I wouldn't dare."

He laughed at that. "This is a cabin, not a museum, so go ahead. I've read it lots of times."

The man loved old books, she marveled as she slid the precious volume from its spot. It only made him more appealing, if that was possible. While she flipped through the heavy parchment pages, she heard cooking-type sounds from around the corner of the staircase that angled its way upstairs. Strolling in, she was surprised by what she found.

Tucked in alongside the original knotty pine cabinets were high-end stainless-steel appliances that would have made a gourmet chef drool with envy. They seemed to be the only change Cooper had made to the cabin, and they stood out like a rocket ship at a hoedown.

"You like to cook?" she asked.

"Oh, yeah," he replied without blinking. "I had my fill of restaurants in New York."

"Huh."

He chuckled. "I take it you're not fond of kitchens."

"My culinary expertise begins and ends with the microwave." She set the treasure of a book on an upper shelf where it would be safe. "Anyone who can cook amazes me."

"Anyone who can write the way you do amazes me."

He added an admiring smile that would have melted the heart of any woman other than her. She'd never lost her head over a guy, and she wasn't about to start now. Still it was a good thing she was devoting all her energy to resuscitating her career, or fending off this one's charms would have been a real challenge.

Eager to move things away from the dangerous personal arena, she examined the back end of his cozy bachelor pad. Another set of wide plank steps led upstairs, and hand-painted waterscapes of the area hung everywhere. But the stunner was the wall of French doors that looked on to the back deck and beyond that, the ocean. If you opened all of them, you could probably hear the waves crashing on the rocks out at the point.

She stood there, drinking in the view, trying to come up with words to adequately describe it. Even with her considerable vocabulary, she couldn't come up with anything better than, "Awesome."

From behind her, Cooper agreed, "Yeah, I like it."

Serene but always in motion, it was the kind of scene that would change from day to day, and season to season. "It must be gorgeous in the fall."

"Now that you know how to get here, you should come back and see for yourself."

Was that a request for a return visit? she wondered. Or was he just making conversation? Apparently Sammy had spotted them at the doors and loped over to join them. Cooper let him in, then filled a large bowl with water. "Here you go, big guy. Lunch was a long time ago, so you must be hungry."

After setting a plate of cheese and crackers on the counter, Cooper rummaged around in the fridge and came up with some leftover meatloaf. Sliding it into the microwave, he chuckled at the dog. "Just don't tell Mom you ate it instead of me. She'd be crushed."

Bree adored the way he talked to the Newfie, and judging by his endlessly wagging tail, Sammy liked it, too. When the timer dinged, he barked eagerly, making her laugh. "I guess he likes meatloaf."

Cooper set the food on the floor, running his hand through the dog's thick fur. "We're a pair, aren't we, boy?"

"You really like him, don't you?" she asked, offering him one of the cheese and cracker sandwiches she'd built.

Taking it, he popped it in his mouth. "What's not to like?"

They chatted about their day while Sammy inhaled his dinner. When there was nothing left on the plate except the checked pattern, he took up his post by one of the French doors, staring longingly outside. Cooper opened the door, and Sammy loped past them and down the dock.

Out on the generous deck, Bree saw Adirondack chairs circled around a sunken fire pit, and a top-of-the-line stainless-steel grill ready for tonight's barbecue. Beneath a wide overhang, a wooden table and chairs were grouped into an outdoor dining room, just waiting for company.

"There he goes," he commented, nodding toward Sammy. Perched on the edge of the dock, the dog studied the water for a few seconds, then dove in. Between the doggy-paddling and slurping, he was kicking up a lot of water, and Cooper laughed. "What a great dog."

"You spent a small fortune getting him groomed," Bree pointed out as she sat in one of the comfy chairs. "Aren't you mad?"

"He's a water dog. Expecting him to stay out of the water would be like expecting you to sit there quietly and not ask me a bunch of questions."

Bree's hackles started to rise. "It's my job to ask people questions."

"Constantly?"

"I ask as many as it takes to get the whole story," she informed him stiffly, echoing her father's mantra. "And then some."

"That's the part they hate most, I'd imagine."

"Lawyers interrogate witnesses all the time. People don't like that much, either."

Sitting crosswise on the chair next to hers, he rested his arms on his knees in a casual pose. "You really like to argue, don't you?"

The twinkle in his eyes told her he was enjoying their little battle, and she went along just for fun. "Well, I don't have a debating trophy or anything…"

When he laughed, she joined him, and the last of her irritation drifted off on the breeze. "Guilty on both counts, I'm afraid. Argumentative *and* nosy."

She'd never admitted that to anyone, she realized, not even herself. It felt strange, but somehow liberating, as if being honest with herself would grow on her if she gave it a chance.

"In your line of work, I'd imagine those are good qualities to have."

"Mostly. Sometimes they get me in trouble, though." That had jumped out of her mouth all on its own, and she cringed at how pathetic it made her sound.

"Everyone makes mistakes, Bree," he said gently. "What we do afterward is what counts."

"I guess." Looking away, she turned her attention to Sammy. Somehow he'd climbed the ladder and stood on the dock, shaking off water before flopping down in an exhausted pile of damp fur. "I'm amazed you want to keep that monster. He's a sweetie, but what's in it for you?"

From the corner of her eye she saw he was focused on the view out to sea and didn't look over. "Sometimes it gets kinda lonely out here. It'd be nice to have someone here when I get home."

"I'm sure there are girls around here who'd love to be here for you."

He groaned. "You sound like my mother. Felicia was the one I wanted to share this with. When she turned me down—"

Cooper shrugged in typical male fashion, but Bree

wasn't letting him get by with that. "That's no excuse for living like a hermit out here. You could keep this place and live in one of those gorgeous houses in town. You'd be closer to your office and—you know—*other people*."

Even she had friends, she added silently. The few solid ones who'd stuck by her and refused to allow her to slide out of touch with them. As far as she knew, Cooper occasionally played golf with Derek Timms and a grown man who still went by the name Otter. That such a great guy would be reaching out to a dog for companionship screamed loneliness to her, and that just seemed wrong.

"Mom and her crew will be here soon," he said, rising from his seat. "If things aren't set up, she'll have my head."

As he went inside, inwardly Bree seethed about the idiocy of the strong silent type. She'd gone out of her way to try to help him, but he wouldn't let her. But when she considered what she'd learned about him, she finally understood where he was coming from.

More than once he'd been betrayed by someone he'd trusted. Loyalty was priceless to Bree, and everything Cooper did and said made it clear he valued it just as highly as she did. While she observed him through the kitchen window, one word came to mind: brokenhearted.

Unfortunately that was a quality she understood very well.

Bree pushed down her own bad memories and tagged after him. She hadn't meant to pry, and his stoic manner made her regret being so inquisitive. Again. She was here to do a job, she reminded herself, not get attached to the people she was writing about.

Especially not this handsome, infuriating man who made her laugh one minute and mutter under her breath the next. The last thing she wanted in her life right now was chemistry. She needed to stay focused on her work, and make sure Nick wouldn't have to think twice about adding her to his permanent staff. Because if things at *Kaleidoscope* didn't work out, her career just might be over.

Chapter Eight

"A few friends, he said," Bree muttered to Amelia while she dumped a tray of empty cups into the trash and replaced them with fresh ones. "There must be two hundred people here."

"It's a great spot to watch the show," she explained, fanning herself with her duster cap. "The only place better is from a boat out in the harbor. Red launches the fireworks from a barge, and with the lighthouse in the background, it's quite a sight."

She'd be stuck here helping clean up, but Bree did her best to sound like a good sport. "It sounds awesome."

"It is," Cooper said from behind her. "I thought you might enjoy seeing it for yourself."

Still holding the tray, she stared at him. "You're going out?"

"Always do."

"And you want to take me with you?"

When he nodded, she felt a rush of excitement and forgot all about being professional. Dropping the cups, she launched herself at him in an impulsive hug. He returned it, and for a few blissful moments, she was wrapped up in those strong arms of his.

Then she realized what she'd done, and she hastily pulled away, hoping no one other than Amelia had noticed. She wasn't keen to become the talk of Holiday Harbor. "Sorry about that. I lost my head there for a second."

"Well, I hate to brag, " he replied, eyes twinkling in fun. "But I'm kind of used to that."

. Rolling her eyes, she decided the best response was to laugh at herself. "I'm sure."

Now that he'd floated the idea, she couldn't wait to go. Not a clock watcher by habit, she couldn't resist checking the display on the microwave every few minutes. At 8:30 p.m., folks started drifting away, headed for the marina. Amelia was one of them, and Cooper came in from the deck to wish his mother good-night.

"Bree, it was lovely to meet you," Amelia said with a warm hug. "If you find yourself back this way, make sure to stop in and see me. There are plenty more Landry stories I didn't get a chance to tell you."

"I'll do that."

Turning to Cooper, Amelia asked, "Dinner at my house tomorrow?"

"Just like every other Tuesday." Giving her an indulgent smile, he walked her to the door and gave her a peck on the cheek. "See you then."

"Such a good boy," she informed Bree. "Believe me, there's not another one like him anywhere. I've looked."

Cooper groaned and gently shoved her onto the front porch. "Good night, Mother."

He closed the door and leaned back against it with

a long-suffering male sigh. "I love her, but she's a real handful sometimes."

"I like her. She's spunky and fascinating to talk to. Not to mention she loves her boy to pieces."

Hanging his head, he grumbled something she didn't catch. But the image of this tall, strapping man being defeated by his slip of a mother made Bree laugh. "Buck up, counselor. She's gone."

Lifting his head, he whined, "Do you have any idea what kind of third degree she'll be giving me at dinner tomorrow?"

Picking up on the legal reference, she suggested, "You could always take the Fifth."

"Not with her. If I don't answer, she'll just make something up."

As he headed for one of the open French doors, she was confused. "We're going now?"

"If you want a good spot, we have to get there soon."

Bree motioned around the wreck that used to be his living room. "Your house is a disaster, and there's still a bunch of people here."

"They all knew I'd be going, and that they're welcome to stay." Reaching back, he snagged a windbreaker from a metal coat tree fashioned to look like a heron. "The place will still be a disaster later, or in the morning. The fireworks are happening now."

"But—"

Shoving the coat at her, he turned on his heel and strode out the door with Sammy in tow. Mumbling about cavemen, she pulled the jacket on and grabbed her camera. Hurrying after him, she noticed he had a pleasant word for everyone they passed by, but not for her. It was like she wasn't even there.

When they got to his boat, though, he stepped in and gallantly offered her a hand. Standing in front of him, she swallowed her pride and thanked him. "I'm kind of a handful, too, aren't I?"

His laughter was a nice switch from the response she normally got from men who'd just discovered how deep her stubborn streak ran. "Yeah, but never boring. That's part of your charm."

While he cast off the lines, she stood there in perplexed silence. She had charm? Since when? Pretty much everyone she'd known for more than five minutes complained about her temper, her intensity or one of several other less-than-appealing qualities. Cooper obviously saw them, but he liked her anyway. Or maybe he was just being nice because he knew she'd be out of his hair in the morning.

Whatever the reason, it was a refreshing change from the usual, and she hummed to herself as she adjusted the settings on her camera for manual photos. Going from near darkness to bright flashes in the sky, it would be tricky getting them just right. She made her best guess and took a few test shots, then adjusted to get a better result. Mostly it kept her from watching Cooper expertly maneuver his boat through the crowded harbor toward an available spot with a straight line of sight to the lighthouse.

By the time they dropped anchor, it was five minutes to nine. Cooper pulled in all the sails, giving them an unobstructed view. All around them boats of various sizes and styles were bobbing in place, their lights twinkling in the slight ripples of the water. The sound of laughter and different styles of music floated on the breeze, giving the night a picnic kind of vibe.

"This is so cool," she said as Cooper joined her on the bench.

"I thought you'd like it." Calling Sammy over, he fastened the offensive leash on to the dog's collar.

The Newfie's face wrinkled into a canine grimace, but he didn't whine. He was being so brave, Bree felt even more sorry for him. "He really hates that. It's like he thinks you don't trust him."

"I know, but if he bolts at the first firecracker, I want to at least have a chance of keeping him in the boat. Finding a black dog in the water at night would be almost impossible."

She had to admit, he made good sense, and she liked the way he guarded the safety of this dog that had appeared in his life. Sammy needed someone to take care of him, to make sure he was safe and happy. Even though Cooper was so busy, she suddenly understood why he hadn't hesitated to adopt the stray.

From taking over his family's firm to spending time with his mother to serving the rest of his grandfather's mayoral term, Cooper took care of things. Not only that, he knew what—and who—was important to him, and gave them the attention they deserved.

Felicia may be gorgeous, rich and famous, Bree concluded, but the model had one severe flaw. She was an idiot to let Cooper Landry get away. Someday some incredibly fortunate woman would become his wife, and Bree hoped his future fiancée would appreciate what she was getting.

Her mulling ended abruptly when she heard the telltale hiss of launching fireworks. Cooper pointed to a section of black sky, and a couple of seconds later, the first sparkler burst to life in the darkness. Several more followed, and then the show was on. There were booming ones, multicolored twists, and some so bright she had to squint to look up at them.

She'd seen plenty of explosive displays, but these were something else again. With the stately lighthouse as a backdrop, it was an incredible sight. A quick check showed her Sammy in the bow of the boat, barking and wagging his tail in approval as each new blast went off. Glancing around, she saw the same appreciation from the people watching Red's show.

Pure, unabashed joy, she thought with a smile. She couldn't recall the last time she'd experienced so much of it in one place. A cool blast of wind coming off the water caught her by surprise, and despite the windbreaker, she folded her arms with a little shiver. Without a word Cooper slipped his jacket off and draped it over her.

Sweet and simple, it was the most wonderful thing anyone had done for her in a very long time. Tilting her head back, she smiled up at him. "Thank you."

"No problem."

"Are you this nice to all the girls, or just me?" He replied with a mischievous grin that made her laugh. "So I'm special?"

"Yup."

Turning to face him, she asked, "Why me? You hardly even know me."

He hesitated for just a second, as if he was weighing whether or not to answer. When he finally spoke, his tone was laced with compassion. "I know you well enough to see you've been kicked around and could use a break."

"Most people don't bother to look that closely at me,"

she confided as the wind picked up and blew her hair into her eyes. "Why do you care?"

Reaching out, he pushed the hair aside with his fingertip and gave her a sympathetic look. "Because you need me to. Isn't that reason enough?"

It was more than reason enough, but the words caught in her throat, and all she could do was nod. He grasped her shoulders, and her heart leaped at the thought that he was moving in to kiss her.

Instead he spun her around and pointed into the sky. "Red's done reloading, so it's time for round two. You don't wanna miss anything."

"Definitely not."

They watched the rest of the fireworks in silence. Oddly, she was both disappointed and relieved that things hadn't gotten romantic. What in the world was wrong with her? Her hands were full just getting her career back on track, she reminded herself sternly. The last thing she needed—or wanted—was the distraction of a relationship, especially this far from civilization. Standing on the gently rocking boat, with Cooper planted solidly behind her, Bree tried to put the near miss out of her mind.

Instead she found herself wishing she could take back what she'd said earlier and invent an excuse to stay in Holiday Harbor.

"Now, you make sure not to be a stranger," Mavis ordered brusquely, cuddling Reggie in her arms while Cooper loaded Bree's bags into his car. "Anytime you want to come back, you'll have a place to stay right here."

Smiling, Bree tickled the pig under his chin the way

he liked and embraced his owner. Though she'd obviously tried to hide it, Mavis had been near tears during breakfast, and Bree wanted to leave her with good memories. "Thanks so much for everything. I've got a whole year's worth of great stories from everything you told me about this place."

The keeper's widow brightened at the compliment. "Maybe you could write a book about Last Chance Lighthouse."

"If I do, I'll dedicate it to you. And Reggie," she added, tapping his snout fondly.

To avoid a long, awkward delay, she waved goodbye and climbed into her seat. Sammy barked "good morning," and she reached back to pet him before buckling in.

Before they crested the hill, she looked back to see Mavis still standing there, silhouetted against the whitewashed walls of the tower that meant so much to her. Choking up a little, Bree waved again, pleased to see the woman smile and return the gesture before disappearing from sight.

It was crazy, Bree knew, but in the past few days, she'd grown very attached to this quaint fishing village and the quirky people who called it home. She'd settle down in a spot like Holiday Harbor someday, she vowed silently. It was a big planet, and there had to be more places like this on it somewhere. She just had to find one of them.

In town things were bustling, and people stopped them every few yards or so to talk to Cooper and his furry new friend. Several wished Bree a good trip home, which she found very sweet. They'd hardly gotten to know her at all, and here they were wishing her well.

Not long ago, she groused, people had been thrilled to see her leaving, because it meant the trouble was over.

When they got to Cooper's office, Bree noticed Julia's storefront was dark, the paper-covered door closed and locked. "Well, that's a bummer," she commented to Cooper. "I was hoping to say goodbye to her in person."

"She's off somewhere, doing something fantastic, no doubt. I'll tell her for you."

"Thanks."

Once they stepped inside the lobby, her tablet displayed a string of messages from Nick in her in-box, and she smiled at the subject lines.

R U working?

Did u get my msg?

Where's my article?

She opened the latest one, sent at the crack of dawn this morning, and typed the only answer she knew he cared about. Coming soon.

After clicking Send, she opened her file to add a description of the Fourth of July in Holiday Harbor. Less than five minutes later, her email alert chimed with his reply: Great job.

Now that she'd gotten positive feedback from him not once but twice, she was feeling better about her future prospects with his magazine.

Pondering her own future led her to another thought, and she waited for Cooper to stop typing before getting his attention. "We've got some time before the bus gets here. Tell me about this development opportunity everyone's so upset about."

"It's probably better if I show you." Spinning around, he took a large cardboard tube from his credenza. While he unrolled the plans, he explained. "Ellington Properties wants to build fifty estate homes around a golf course out at Schooner Point. To start."

He anchored the top corners with a stapler and tape dispenser, holding the others down with his fists. It was a furious pose, and Bree couldn't help staring at him. Gone was the calm, composed demeanor she'd assumed was his nature. As he glared at the plans, his eyes blazed like furious sapphires, sharp and dangerous.

"You don't like this idea?" she asked, even though the answer was obvious.

That got her a derisive laugh completely out of character for the easygoing man she'd spent the weekend getting to know. Summoning a patient tone, she asked, "May I see?"

"Don't get all polite on me. If you want to look, go ahead."

The date on the plans was almost a year ago, which didn't make sense. "These are dated last fall. Why are you only voting about it now?"

"Because I didn't know anything about it till I was hunting for something in Granddad's office and found this wedged inside a drawer." His voice still hummed with barely contained anger, and she could only imagine how furious he'd been when he'd first uncovered the drawings.

Choosing her words carefully, she asked, "Are you mad because you hate the idea or because your grandfather kept it a secret?"

Cooper opened his mouth immediately, then closed it just as quickly. Giving her something between a grimace and a grin, through clenched teeth, he ground out, "Both."

"I don't get it. Why would he do that?"

"His family's been here forever, and he loved this place just the way it was. It might not be perfect, but it's our home. He wouldn't want anyone to change it, no matter how good their ideas look on paper."

The truth of it was, his beloved grandfather had played judge and jury on this one, and now Cooper was left holding the bag. Bree suspected he felt the same way, whether he'd admit it or not. She examined the oversize pages more carefully. "Where's Schooner Point?"

"Out on the bluff, not far from the Captains' Chapel. It overlooks the harbor on one side and the ocean on the other." He pointed to the plans. "The length of the eighteenth hole they want to build overlooks the water, like at Pebble Beach in California."

Her first thought was that this developer really knew his stuff. No doubt he was aware of the perilous financial situation in Holiday Harbor, and that land values were way down from their peaks years ago. All he had to do was offer 10 percent more than their most recent assessments, and he'd have all the land he needed for his luxury community. The vacant land would come even cheaper.

The wheels in Bree's head were spinning full-tilt, and she could barely contain her excitement. This was the kind of story she lived for, the kind she needed now more than ever. She could imagine the headline in a large-impact font, right above her byline.

Winners and Losers: Small-Town America Versus Corporate America.

While the potential development angle was a great concept for another series of articles, she recognized the trouble it would probably cause Holiday Harbor and its reluctant mayor. Cooper had made his position clear, but she couldn't help wondering how the other residents in town were planning to vote.

Then again, overextending her professional boundaries was what had gotten her sentenced to journalistic Siberia in the first place. She'd just started to get back on her feet careerwise, and she couldn't afford any more missteps. Maybe the key to continuing that success was to conceal her own views until she had the whole story. It was worth a shot, anyway.

"I'm sure your grandfather thought he was doing what was best," she amended, "but I'm glad you're giving everyone a chance to weigh in on this project. It could save Holiday Harbor."

"Or destroy it."

"Change isn't always bad, Cooper," she reasoned. "More people in town means more money spent in the stores, more kids in the schools, more taxes for maintaining roads and bringing in better technology. Can you imagine how much the property taxes would be for homes like these?"

"A private golf community, with everything they need inside the gates they'll use to keep out the riffraff," he predicted darkly. "As one of the folks they'll be locking out, I object."

"You're not riffraff," she chided, waving away the idea. "Besides, I thought you liked golfing."

"It's not the course I object to," he explained. "It's the

houses. I've known more than my share of people who think they're better than everyone else. I came home to get away from all that."

He had a point, but it was Bree's job to remain objective and start compiling facts, not give in to emotion. "How many houses are up there now?"

Checking the schematic, he shrugged. "Ten or twelve, I guess."

"And the rest is undeveloped land?"

His hesitation was answer enough, but she waited for him to respond. "Just because it's not being used doesn't mean it doesn't have value. It's wild and beautiful up there, just the way God made it. It should stay that way."

The conviction in his tone wobbled as he glanced back at the plans. Cooper might not have concrete figures, but he must have some concept of how much money was poised to flood into his struggling hometown.

Because she was on her way back to Richmond, Bree had no business getting involved in this issue. When her life had come crashing down around her, she'd vowed to never again stick her nose in where it didn't belong. But for some reason, now she felt compelled to do exactly that. "You're voting on this at the town meeting later this month, right?"

His eyes narrowed suspiciously, but he nodded. "Why?"

"Oh, you know me," she said with a smile. "Just curious."

Chapter Nine

The offhand remark struck him oddly, and Cooper eyed her with suspicion. "Right."

"You're a smart guy, and I know you'll figure it out. No matter how bad things might look now, Holiday Harbor won't fade away like Sandy Cove did."

That trip had really affected her, and he was pleased to see she hadn't forgotten it. Then again, how could she when Sammy was a furry memento of what they'd experienced there? That reminded him of something he'd been meaning to ask her. "The story you did about Sammy. Can I still read it online?"

"Sure. It's had so many hits, Nick's going to leave it up all week as a freebie. After that, you'll have to pay for it, though," she added with a wink.

"Great. Meantime, I have a couple things to do before the bus comes in. Do you mind waiting for me?"

"Oh, you don't have to go with me. It's just down the street."

"I met you when you came in, I'll walk you out. Besides," he added with a grin, "if I don't go, how will I get my goodbye kiss?"

"Who said anything about a kiss?" she shot back, but the mischievous twinkle in her eyes gave her away.

As she slid her ear buds in and picked up her tablet, he couldn't help laughing. One thing her future boyfriend could be sure of, he thought as he rolled up the offensive plans and stowed them in the box. Their life together would never be boring.

When Cooper was finished, he realized she'd been in his office for nearly two hours that morning, but she was so quiet, he'd barely noticed her. While he'd made some phone calls and tapped away on his keyboard, the virtual keys on her tablet made no noise at all.

Was that how she lived all the time? he wondered. Shrinking into a corner so she was all but invisible, observing what went on around her but not participating in it? She had a masterful touch with people, but she seemed to be able to turn it on and off at will. It made him more curious than ever about what actually went on in that sharp mind of hers.

Unfortunately he wasn't likely to learn any more about her than he already had. Despite her apparent fondness for his town, once she left he'd probably never see her again.

When he slid his chair out, Sammy cracked one eye open to look up as Cooper stood and stretched his back. "Ready to go?"

Sammy jumped to his feet, but Bree didn't react, so Cooper strolled over and lightly tapped her shoulder. She bolted from the couch as if he'd shot her, the cord from her ear buds dangling between them.

"Don't do that!" she scolded, pulling them loose. "You almost gave me a heart attack."

Cooper had never met someone who concentrated so

intently, almost as if she was lost in another world. Holding up his hands to calm her, he said, "I didn't mean to scare you, but it's quarter to eleven. We should get you down to the bus stop."

"You're kidding." She blinked at him, then glanced out the window. "You're not kidding. Wow, where'd the morning get to?"

He took her beat-up messenger bag from the chair where she'd dropped it and handed it to her. "You've been working like crazy. Sammy and I went out for a walk, but you never moved. I'd be a pretzel if I sat like that for so long."

She spun from side to side, and her back cracked with the movement. "I'm pretty close to it myself."

Mrs. Andrews nodded to them on their way out, and Cooper managed to convince Bree to let him carry everything but her messenger bag. As they walked toward the waiting bus, he noticed the shops were fairly busy, and The Albatross was full up, with diners waiting on the benches out front. The cries of gulls and terns overhead mingled with the sounds of people talking, punctuated by frequent laughter. It was an enjoyable, relaxed scene, and he was proud of what he saw. If only the other side of the street was as busy, he'd be a happy man.

Somehow, he vowed silently, they'd figure out a way to make it happen. And then he could tell the next developer who came sniffing around to build his fancy golf course community somewhere else.

"How long has Julia Stanton been here?" Bree asked, pulling his attention back to reality.

"She came to town this spring on vacation and decided to move here. I handled the closing on the property for her."

"She bought the whole building? Isn't that kind of unusual?"

Cooper couldn't understand why she was so curious, but then this was Bree. In the short time he'd known her, he'd come to accept that she was interested in everything that went on around her. "Not really. There's a nice apartment upstairs, and the store below. It's a good setup, especially in the winter."

"I can't argue with that."

For some reason her doubtful tone irked him. Up to this point, her visit had been a roller coaster of highs and lows, and he didn't want to end it with an argument. So he kept quiet, and they walked the rest of the way in silence. He wasn't sure if he was going to miss her or couldn't wait for her to leave. Like an unpredictable storm, she'd blown into his nice quiet life and turned it into something he barely recognized.

In only five days. He hated to consider the damage she could have done if she'd stayed any longer.

Just as they reached the curb where the bus was parked, Bree's phone rang. Checking the caller ID, she gave Cooper a sly smile and hit the answer button. "Nick, thanks for getting back to me. Cooper's here, so I put you on speaker."

"Where are you?"

"The bus stop."

"I got your email. I want you to stay and cover the development vote, use some more of your Sandy Cove research to show the readers what's at stake for Holiday Harbor. Got it?"

"Got it."

She clicked the phone off, and Cooper's temper spiked almost immediately. Taking a deep breath, he cautioned himself that the sidewalks were full of people who had no business hearing what he was about to say. "You told him?"

He was certain she'd relayed the gist of the Ellington Properties proposal to Nick, and it didn't thrill him to know their private conversation had left his office. For her part, she shrugged as if it didn't matter in the least. "It's a big story. I emailed him what I knew, figuring he could decide if he wanted me to cover it or not."

"I don't want it covered," Cooper protested in a hushed voice, although he had a feeling it was pointless. Since Nick had gotten back to her this quickly, the editor's strategy was obvious. Excitement equaled readers. Apparently that was all these two cared about.

"It's not your call this time. It's mine." For emphasis she tapped the phone against her faded Yankees T-shirt. "And I'm gonna get to work."

With that she took out her steno pad and calmly strolled in the other direction. Cooper had the sinking feeling that the development vote wasn't the only challenge headed his way.

The other was somehow coping with the fact that this sassy, irresistible woman was no longer on her way back to Virginia.

"You've got a nice hand with the wheel, little lady," Jack told Bree while she carefully guided his fishing boat toward the wharf. "Wish my own kids had half your feel for it."

She'd been out on the water with Jack and his crew all day, and the praise settled pleasantly into her tired brain. During her shift she'd learned his last name was

Walters, and way more than she needed to know about how and where to pull in nets full of Atlantic mackerel.

Jack had generously invited Sammy along, and the Newfie was having a blast, racing up and down the decks with Jack's terrier, Horatio. Their size difference didn't seem to matter to them, and they became quick friends. When their hectic day was over, they'd probably drop from exhaustion when they got home.

The cook hollered, "Snack time for mutts!" and the two dogs trotted past her on their way to the galley. Her camera was out of reach, so she committed the chummy picture to memory. "Thanks for the compliment. I'm not sure I could do this every day like you guys, but I learned a lot."

"Ah, there's the rub. It's more than a job, for sure, driven by what's in here." Resting a battered hand on his wide chest, he grinned and lifted a finger to his temple. "Not in here. If I had any sense at all, I'd have given it up when I was in high school."

"Why didn't you?" she asked, nudging the wheel to stay in line with the buoys that marked the lane in from the ocean. On first glance they looked like they were just bobbing in place, with no rhyme or reason. Now that she'd attended Jack's Piloting 101, she could see they formed a broken line in the water.

"What? And work eight to five locked up in a factory somewhere? Lining some fat cat's pockets while I watched the clock and worried about how my retirement fund was doing? Don't think so."

Bree hadn't gotten a firm handle on his age before, and she wasn't any closer to it now. Even hushed questions about it to his crew had left her nowhere. Sensing an opening, she took another shot. "But you have to retire sometime, right? I mean, you can't work forever."

"Says you," he retorted with a roguish grin. "When the Good Lord calls me home, they'll be hauling me off the *Brenda* in a pine box."

"Your wife, Brenda, might be glad to have you home more, though."

"Nah. I'd just be underfoot. Trust me on this one, a marriage works best when a husband and wife have their own space. Keeps the fighting to a minimum."

Getting relationship advice from this burly fisherman struck her as funny, and she laughed. "If I ever find myself in that situation, I'll remember that."

"Oh, you won't be single forever," he predicted. "Smart, pretty thing like you? Not a chance."

If he wasn't married, and a full eighteen inches taller than her, she'd have hugged the old coot. Instead she settled for a warm smile. "You probably say that to all the girls."

"Only if it's true," he assured her with a wink. Suddenly his gray eyes took on a steely glare, and he bellowed, "Grover!"

His sunburned first mate peered in through the starboard window. "Yeah, boss?"

"My eyes ain't what they used to be." He nodded toward the wharf. "Look up there and tell me what you see."

Grover complied, and his scowl was just as threatening as Jack's glare. "There's a fancy yellow-and-white yacht tied up in your slip, boss."

"With a sign marked for the *Brenda,* plain as day." The captain growled like an unhappy bear. "I've had enough of these playtime fishermen interfering with my business. Hand that wheel over, missy, and no matter what happens, stay put. This could get nasty."

While she knew he'd never harm her, she didn't waste any time getting out of his way. Scrambling onto the aft deck, she sent an urgent text to Cooper.

SOS—trouble at docks.

He knew she was out with Jack, and she hoped Cooper would be able to defuse the situation before things got out of hand. When Sammy appeared at her side near the rail, she absently patted his head while her mind sifted through possible scenarios. She couldn't just stand aside and let these guys pound on each other. If all else failed, she finally decided, she'd scream and pretend to faint. Not the most dignified plan, but it should get everyone's attention.

Jack seemed to be coming in at the completely wrong angle, parallel to the docks. She was flabbergasted when he brought the trawler to a stop a few yards from the offending yacht.

Calling for a couple spare hands, he ordered two of his men to toss in their mooring ropes and pull in as close to the pier as they could. When they were tied off, he clambered onto the rail, then up the emergency ladder that led up from the water. Then, as if he did it every day, he calmly strode up the dock. It was like something straight out of an old swashbuckling movie, and Bree had a hard time believing the old sailor had managed it.

One by one his crew followed suit, until there was a line of grimy men moving toward the offending boat. Bree's instinct was to trail after them, but she knew if he saw her up there, Jack wouldn't be happy. Right now seemed like a bad time to test his patience.

Arms crossed, Jack stood with his legs apart wide and yelled, "Ahoy, *Daisy Mae!*"

As if on cue, everyone stopped what they were doing and turned to watch the unfolding scene. It was so quiet, Bree could hear the bell on a marker far out to sea.

A slender man on deck turned in surprise, frowning when he saw Jack, his men standing in a half-circle formation behind him. "Can I help you?"

"You're in my space, son."

"It's the only empty one."

"There's a few right over there." Jack nodded toward the other side of the wharf. "We save 'em for our guests."

"I'm meeting friends for dinner, and I'm already late," the moron snapped as he walked onto the gangway. "I don't have time to move it now."

"No need to trouble yourself. Grover here can move her for you."

Grover hurried forward, saluting Jack as he jogged past. The smug visitor dangled his key chain. "I don't think so."

"Aw, that's nothin'," Jack assured him. "Grover don't need keys to start a boat."

The man whipped around just as the sailor swung onto the deck and made for the stairs leading to the fancy wheelhouse. As the thought of someone hotwiring his precious boat sank in, the man pointed a threatening finger at Jack. "Call him off, or we'll have a serious problem, old man."

The taunt backfired, and a calm but very determined Jack sauntered up to meet their visitor in the middle of the dock.

Fortunately so did Cooper.

Offering his hand to the intruder, he hauled out that disarming lawyer's smile. "Cooper Landry, mayor of Holiday Harbor."

"Kevin Dearborn."

When he eyed Jack expectantly, the old salt chortled. "Not a chance. You can just call me 'sir.'"

Bree smothered a laugh with her hand, but Cooper's sharp ears caught her squeak, and he glanced her way. When she sent him an apologetic look, his mouth quirked in an almost-grin before he turned back to the two arguing men. "Why don't you tell me what's going on? Maybe I can help."

Jack motioned for Kevin to start, which she thought was nice of him, considering the situation. Then she realized it was because Cooper understood the problem, and Jack wasn't going to waste his breath telling the mayor something he already knew.

This had happened before, she realized, recalling Jack's violent reaction to the *Daisy Mae* and his criticism of sports fishermen her first night in town. So tourism had its downside, too. It shed new light on the town's decline, and how crucial it was to come up with a solution everyone could live with. Her assignment had just gone from puff piece to the kind of gritty, hard-hitting journalism she thrived on.

When Kevin was finished relaying his side of the story, he pointed over. "He sent one of his guys onto my boat. I want him off."

"No problem." Jack let out a piercing whistle, and the crazy first mate saluted from the wheelhouse. Coming out on the walkway, he did a nice half pike into the water, and the fascinated crowd burst into laughing applause. If they'd had judging paddles, she suspected they'd have given him a perfect score.

"This place is nuts," Kevin said, and not in a nice way. "Stay off my boat, or I'll have you arrested."

Instead of delivering his threat and walking away like a smart person would have done, he made the mistake of poking Jack in the chest. The captain grabbed his hand and flung it away in one powerful motion. "Touch me again, I'll put you in the drink with Grover."

Kevin turned to Cooper with a pleading look. "You're supposed to be in charge of these lunatics. Aren't you going to do something?"

"Seems to me things are under control." Turning to Jack, he asked, "Wouldn't you say so?"

"Yup. No problems here."

Kevin's eyes narrowed in fury, and he spat, "You'll be hearing from my lawyer."

As he turned to go, Cooper caught his arm. Taking a business card from his jacket's chest pocket, he grinned. "I'll be looking forward to speaking with him soon. In the meantime you need to move your boat so the crew can process their catch while it's fresh."

"I'm already late for dinner."

"So'm I," Jack rumbled, "but I got a few tons of fish to unload first. If it wasn't for guys like me, you and your friends'd be eating salad and rolls tonight."

Kevin seemed ready to continue arguing, but a quick look at the unyielding fisherman and the tall man in the suit apparently changed his mind. Without a word he stalked back to his boat and glided over to remoor where he should have been in the first place. It took him less than five minutes.

When the fuss was over, Cooper strolled over to the *Brenda* and gazed down at Bree and Sammy. "What're you doing down there?"

"Jack told me to stay put, and I figured it was a good idea to listen to him."

"Really?" he teased as he reached a hand down to bring her onto the dock. "I'll have to find out his secret."

Once they'd rescued Sammy and Horatio, she asked, "Do you really think Dearborn will sic his lawyer on you?"

"I hope he does. We get a few of these arrogant jerks every summer, and everyone's tired of it. I don't care how much money he's got. Nobody comes into this town and shoves aside the people who built it."

The protectiveness in his voice got her attention, and she gained a new level of respect for the reserved lawyer. It was inspiring to meet someone who stood up for what they believed in, no matter how much trouble it caused. "Those reserved signs don't work."

"I know. Folks who aren't from around here think they're just for fun, I guess."

"Jack's pretty reasonable, but some of the other captains, not so much. If you don't do something, someone's gonna get hurt."

"Tell me something I don't know," he muttered.

Searching for answers, Bree glanced around the bustling pier. When her eyes landed on the unused section, a lightbulb went off. "Maybe you could refurbish that side for pleasure boats, and keep them out of the crews' way."

"I'd love to, but we just don't have the money."

"You would," she pointed out, "if you approved Ellington's plan and got those big houses on the tax rolls."

Shoving his hands deep into his pockets, he sighed. "I know. I'm just worried about what it'd cost us in the long run."

The night of the development vote the town meeting was packed.

Cooper did a quick count of rows and multiplied that by the number of occupied chairs in each row. Five hundred, more than double their usual attendance, and max capacity for their modest town hall. At least everyone was taking this thing seriously.

Bree sat in the back corner, tucked behind a dusty blackboard so no one would notice her. She'd told him she wanted to capture the give and take of the normal meeting and contrast that with the emotions the contentious vote was liable to unleash.

Cooper called the meeting to order right on time. There were a few business-related issues, such as who was responsible for fixing the cracked sidewalk between two shops. The grocer's wife bemoaned the loss of her prize-winning begonias to a rogue mutt with a taste for fresh flowers. Cooper managed to keep a straight face while reminding everyone of the leash law.

That brought a ripple of laughter, and a few glanced back at Sammy, stretched out in his spot next to Bree's chair. Grinning, she held up her end of the leash, which made everyone laugh again. It was a tight, nervous sound, as if they all sensed this was the calm before the storm.

Bringing the routine business to a close, Cooper took a deep breath and said, "Now for why we're all really here. At last month's meeting, I presented a plan from Ellington Properties, a real estate development firm interested in building a golf course community out at Schooner Point. Before we adjourn to vote on it, I wanted to go over the high points of the proposal again and answer any questions you might have."

The room was silent until he finished outlining the developer's offer. When he indicated he was done, the place erupted.

"Not in this lifetime!" one man insisted.

"This is just what we've been praying for," another said more quietly. "Now we can afford to retire and move closer to our grandchildren."

That was just the beginning of a spirited back and forth. By his estimation, half the people loved the idea and would have signed on the dotted line if the contracts had been sitting on the table. The other half hated it with a passion Cooper found more than a little disturbing.

Trapped in the middle of the skirmish, he dutifully stayed at the lectern, feeling like a condemned man waiting to discover whether he'd be hung or beheaded. He hadn't asked for any of this, yet here he was, doing his best to make sure everyone's opinion was heard.

Finally Jack stood and turned to address his neighbors. "I don't know about all o' you, but I'd like to hear what our mayor has to say about this."

Several shouted agreement, and Cooper faced them squarely, careful to keep his expression neutral. "I want what's best for our town. This is a very important decision, and we need to make it carefully." He looked around the crowded hall, connecting with several sets of eyes, some angry, others sympathetic. "All of us together."

"But what do you think of the proposal?" a softer

voice asked. He spotted Julia Stanton standing at the end of a middle row, her face lined with concern.

"We've known for a while that we need to replace the revenue we're losing from our fishing industry," he replied evenly. "I think the best option is to get more tourists in here. That way we're only renting out part of the town during the nicest months. Over the winter we'd have it all to ourselves again."

"Except for those nutty ice fishermen," someone commented, his laughter breaking some of the tension.

Several residents popped up with questions or concerns, and the occasional "Let's do it!" Beneath it all was a rumble of several unrelated conversations he wished he could follow. Then again, he might be better off not knowing.

Cooper let them air their comments, only stepping in when someone talked over someone else or ridiculed a differing view. After nearly an hour he held up his hands for quiet. "All right, then. It's getting late, so let's wind this up so we can all vote and head on home. By the way, anyone who turns in a ballot gets a free piece of pie, courtesy of the Captains' Chapel Ladies' Aid."

His announcement brought a round of applause, and everyone stood to fold up their chairs and stack them against the walls. While they got themselves arranged in a fairly orderly line, Cooper strolled back to where Bree was finishing up her notes. He paused next to her chair, taking Sammy's leash from her so she could uncoil herself from what he'd come to think of as her pretzel position.

"Impressive, Mr. Mayor," she approved, sliding her tablet into her ever-present messenger bag. "You let them know how you feel without actually saying you oppose developing Schooner Point. Must be all that courtroom practice you've had."

The way she said it, it sounded like a compliment, and he decided to take it that way. "Guess so."

"Cooper." Heeding the emphasis in her tone, he met those dark, intelligent eyes. "Everything will work out, one way or another. You'll see."

For lack of anything better, he smiled and held open the swinging door for her to leave. Her phone rang, and she paused in the entryway to check the caller. "It's my mom. This signal's much better than the one at the lighthouse. Is it okay if I just hang out here and talk to her?"

"Sure. Just don't do any exit polling."

"Me?" Blinking, she gave him an innocent smile. "I'd never even think of it."

"I mean it, Bree," he replied in a more serious tone. "Voting's private, and I don't want anyone to get the idea you're gonna put the details online for the whole word to see."

In a heartbeat her joking demeanor shifted to one that more closely matched his own. "I understand, and I'll report just the results, not people's individual comments. You have my word on it."

Not long ago this reporter's word would have meant less than nothing to him. But over the past couple of weeks, he'd grown to trust her more and more, and he was confident she'd stand by her promise.

"Okay. Have a good night."

As he walked Sammy back inside, one thing was clear to him. Progress had come to Holiday Harbor. The big question was would they embrace it, or turn it away?

* * *

While everyone was distracted with the hubbub of the voting, Bree quietly chatted with her mom. After catching her up on what had become a fascinating assignment, Bree hung up and got ready to leave. Then she realized she could see and hear everything going on inside and decided to stay right where she was. The alcove under the coat rack was dark, so no one could see her. Cooper would probably kill her for doing this, but she'd deal with that later. If he found out, that is. If he didn't, no harm done, and she'd keep her change in plans to herself.

One thing she wouldn't even consider doing was breaking her promise to guard the voters' privacy. While it was tempting to ferret out some emotional reactions to the night's events, no story in the world was worth losing Cooper's respect. Proud of herself for doing the right thing, she observed what she could from her sheltered spot.

One of the entryway doors was missing, which gave her a decent view of the long table that held two boxes. They weren't marked, so people wouldn't know what their neighbors had written on their folded slips of paper. It wasn't exactly cutting edge, but it worked fine. Cooper stood off to the side, talking with Derek and some of the business owners, trying to look cool when she knew his stomach must be in knots.

As people cast their ballots and dug into their yummy-looking rewards, Bree's own stomach began to growl. Rummaging around in her bag, she found half of a candy bar. The stale half. She munched on it to pass the time, and gradually the din inside the large open room tapered off to just a few voices. Among them she clearly heard Cooper and Derek, discussing their next round of golf with Otter tomorrow.

By nine-thirty, all the votes had been tallied. Three hundred for, three hundred against. Based on her interviews around town, Bree wasn't surprised in the least, and she leaned out to get a better view of the main hall.

Now the boxes were labeled Yes and No. Sitting at the table where Derek and three others had been counting, Cooper flung his head back and glared at the arched ceiling. With a groan, he swiveled his head to look at Derek. "You're kidding, right?"

Grimacing, his old friend shook his head. "We counted 'em three times, and it was the same every round. As mayor, the bylaws say you have to break the tie."

"Pay attention, buddy," Cooper grumbled as he scribbled his choice on a slip of paper. "This is the kind of trouble you're in for."

Cooper handed the paper to him, and Derek hesitated. "Don't you want to do that in private?"

"It won't matter." He checked his watch. "By ten, everyone will know it was a draw, and I had to break it. Even if they missed the point that I'm completely against this project, when they hear the results they'll know I voted against developing Schooner Point."

Shrugging, Derek added the folded paper to the "no" pile. "Okay, but don't say I didn't give you a chance."

"Duly noted." Standing, Cooper shook hands with his friend. "It's been a long day, so I'm headed home. My house phone'll be off the hook, so if you really need me, call my cell."

"Good idea. These folks—" he rattled the "yes" box "—won't be thrilled with you."

Cooper chuckled. "Once you're mayor, I'm looking forward to not worrying about that kind of nonsense anymore. Night."

"Night."

Bree expected Derek to follow him out, but for some reason he didn't. Instinct told her to stay put, so she shrank back a little farther into the darkness and waited. She heard a side door close, then Derek's footsteps as he walked back through the empty hall. The telltale beeps of a phone dialing broke the silence, and she strained her ears to catch what was going on.

"Just calling to tell you the vote went exactly the way I predicted." He paused, then said, "No, it's not a problem. After the special election on Labor Day, I'll be mayor, and this will all be moot. We'll tweak your proposal and reissue it for another vote. Some of these folks are on the fence already, and with a little arm-twisting, we'll have enough support to avoid another tie. We'll be breaking ground for those big beautiful houses by fall, just like I promised. Partner."

Bree's jaw fell open, and she was glad she was sitting down or she might have dropped from shock. Derek didn't oppose the development as he claimed. He was in the developer's pocket, trading his influence with the locals for a piece of the action. Intentionally deceiving everyone, putting Holiday Harbor at risk so he could make a fortune for himself.

And Cooper had no idea.

He'd said it more than once: he didn't want to be mayor. Since he believed Derek's vision for the town's future matched his own, he was happy to turn the position over to a man he'd known and trusted since childhood. With Cooper's history, she knew this latest betrayal would break his big generous heart. She certainly wasn't thrilled about being the messenger, especially when the only proof she had was half a conversation she shouldn't have heard in the first place.

Technically she was just a reporter from out of town, and this had absolutely nothing to do with her. If she'd left the meeting when she was supposed to, she wouldn't know anything about Derek's plan. Her confrontation with the kindly senator earlier that year still rankled in her memory, and she wasn't eager for a repeat performance. It was possible she'd misunderstood this situation, too, and if she said anything the result would be even more damaging. Because then she'd risk losing Cooper's friendship, and that would be a hundred times worse.

Biting back a moan, she rested her head against the wall and wondered. Should she wade into the middle of this mess? Or was this one of those times when a smart girl would just walk away?

Chapter Ten

That Sunday was even more interesting than usual at the Captains' Chapel. The entire congregation, Bree included, showed up wearing their grungiest work clothes. Pastor Allen's sermons were always good, but this one was the best so far. Smiling throughout, he praised them for giving their time and energy to the church's annual painting job.

"God's house is more than four walls and a roof," he concluded proudly. "All of us together make it what He meant for it to be: a place to gather and connect with our neighbors. When we do, we learn more about each other, and that we're really not that different, after all."

With that, he ended the service, and people streamed out to get to work. Bree hung back, and when Cooper noticed, he turned to her with a confused look.

"Aren't you coming?" he asked.

Actually, since the town meeting she'd been trying to avoid him without seeming like she was avoiding him. As observant as he was, he'd notice something was bugging her, and he'd want to know what it was. Beyond that she felt awful for keeping Derek's apparent betrayal from Cooper. She'd always been up front with him, even when it made her cringe. Staying quiet about such a huge secret didn't feel right to her, but she didn't want to start trouble unless she was 100 percent certain of her facts.

"I don't want to be in the way while you're setting up." Evading his gaze, she fiddled with the settings on her camera. "I'll be out in a minute."

Apparently that wasn't good enough for him, and he stayed until the last of the group had left the sanctuary. Coming closer, he stopped just short of where Bree stood and waited. When she refused to lift her eyes, he gently tipped her chin up with his finger. "Are you okay?"

The intimate gesture was so unexpected, she felt her jaw drop open in surprise. "You're worried about me?"

"You look like you haven't slept in days. What's going on?"

She simply couldn't lie to this man. Scrambling for words, she came up with something that was more or less the truth. "I'm having trouble with some details for my development article, that's all."

His frown eased a little, but he asked, "Anything I can help with?"

Typical Cooper, she thought with a smile. Always riding in to save the day. "Not really, but thanks for the offer."

"Anytime."

Grinning now, he stepped back to let her leave the church ahead of him. Even while she walked out, she felt his strong, protective presence behind her. She'd dated guys who were more guards than boyfriends, to the point of smothering her. She'd also known some who couldn't have cared less what she did. Or how well she'd been sleeping.

Then there was Cooper. Bree didn't doubt that when he finally found a woman to share the rest of his life with, he'd devise a way to shield her from the big bad world, without strangling her in the process. Bree had to admit, she was jealous of the future Mrs. Landry, and the woman didn't even exist yet.

Shaking herself free of her pointless brooding, Bree took up residence on a vacant picnic table to watch Red Granger organize the volunteers. Consulting a paint-spattered clipboard, he found a job for everyone, from his ninety-year-old mother to toddlers who couldn't do much besides fetch lemonade. Several guys lugged picnic tables farther out of the painting zone, and members of the Ladies' Aid spread a lavish picnic over them. Pastor Allen got two enormous grills started, announcing that he'd cook the meat at noon. Every member of the congregation was involved in some way, and she found that endearing for some reason.

She was snapping photos when Mavis stepped in front of her viewfinder. "What're you doing?"

"Documenting things for tomorrow's installment."

Scowling, the gruff woman pointed to an empty spot on one wall. "I need another set of hands in my section."

"Oh, Mavis." Bree laughed. "I'm more the call-the-landlord kind of girl. I've never painted in my life."

Mavis folded her arms in stark disapproval. "You ever scrape a label off your windshield?"

"Sure."

In reply Mavis handed her a wide scraper and went back the way she'd come. Well and truly shanghaied, Bree stowed her camera and trailed after her foreman.

Georgia and Carolina, the bakery owners, were kind enough to show her the basic motion. After a few tries Bree managed to remove only the loose paint and not a chunk of the clapboards.

Several others were doing the same thing, and they all chatted pleasantly while they worked. Gossip flew on the warm breeze, and she snagged a few tidbits she'd never print but were entertaining, all the same.

During a lemonade break, she asked, "How often do you guys do this?"

"Every year," the Southern sisters replied in tandem. They did that constantly, and at first Bree had considered it more than a little odd. She was used to it now, so she didn't think anything of it.

"Salt air's tough on the paint," Mavis added. "If we don't keep up with the maintenance, this place'll rot where it stands."

"You could put on vinyl siding," Bree suggested sensibly. "That way the wood would be protected but you wouldn't ever have to paint again."

"Not as long as I'm on the church council," Mavis retorted. "This chapel's been here a long time, and it's fine just the way it is."

"Besides," Carolina said more gently, "we enjoy our working picnics. It brings us all together, doing something for our church. I can't think of a better way to spend a Sunday."

"Well said," her sister agreed, raising her lemonade for a toast. "To the Captains' Chapel. May it always be a fitting home for God's children."

They all chimed in with an Amen, and Bree was stunned to hear her own voice among them. Even more stunning was the fact that she hadn't merely parroted their response. She meant it with all her heart.

In that moment the knotted thoughts that had kept her awake all night fell loose, and she knew what she had to do. It wouldn't be easy, but she had to find a way. These were good people, and they deserved better than what Derek had in mind for them.

Looking into the flawless blue sky, she sent up a silent prayer for strength. Normally she took great pride in doing things on her own, but this time she'd need all the help she could get.

By the time Bree finished her spy's tale, Mavis was glowering over the rim of her teacup. "Traitor."

"Hey, it's not my fault! I'm just the messenger."

Mavis looked confused, then comprehension softened her stern expression. Reaching over, she patted Bree's hand in a comforting gesture that seemed strange coming from the brusque keeper's widow. "Not you, honey. I was talking about that no-good traitor Derek."

That was a relief. The vengeful gleam in her hostess's eyes was making her nervous, so she quickly got back on track. "I wasn't supposed to be there, and Cooper will probably be furious with me for eavesdropping. But this is important, and I have to tell him. I just don't know how."

"You're right, on all counts." Mavis sighed, the deep lines on her face bracketing her disappointment. "Those two boys have been thick as thieves since they were babies. I never thought much of that Timms whelp, but I can't believe he'd sell out his own town like this."

"Maybe he needs the money," Bree suggested. "Did he take out loans for Yale?"

"And then some. But he was bent on following Cooper, so he did. Never did half as well, though," she added proudly, as if it was her own son's accomplishment.

"Then there's his fancy car, and starting up his own firm. It could be he's strapped for cash."

"So'm I," Mavis retorted with venom. "You don't see me makin' shady deals with no-good mansion builders set on destroying this place."

"I wasn't making excuses for him, just thinking out loud. What he's trying to do is wrong, and someone has to stop him. The problem is, I'm the only one who knows what he's up to, and I didn't exactly walk up and ask him about it openly."

"This ain't a court of law. You heard what you heard, and it's up to you to tell Cooper."

Bree did some scowling of her own. "He won't believe me. At least not at first."

"Then you have to convince him. When he sees what's going on behind his back, I know he'll do the right thing."

"Which is what?"

"Run for mayor," she replied immediately. "Stop this nonsense before it gets outta hand."

"There's no way to get him on the ballot now. He would've had to declare his candidacy months ago."

Her logic didn't faze Mavis in the least. "We've written in folks before. We'll do it again."

"But he doesn't want to be mayor," Bree pointed out. "He never did."

"I know that, but we needed him, and he agreed to do it." Another proud smile. "Cooper Landry's the kind of man who always steps up and does what's right. He won't let us down."

During her time in Holiday Harbor, Bree had watched him do just that, time after time. Whether it was saving a dog that needed a home or presiding fairly over an issue that tore him apart inside, he did what was best. But before she went to him with something this explosive, she needed more than a few words overheard from a dark hallway.

She needed proof. She just had to figure out how to get it.

"No."

In her shop Monday morning, Julia emphatically shook her head, her teardrop sapphire earrings jangling their own protest. Turning partially away, she put a little more energy into ripping open a box of office supplies than was strictly necessary. Pausing midtear, she gazed at Bree with a stricken expression. "We've spent a lot of time together, and I thought we were friends. How could you ask me to do something like this?"

"*Because* we're friends." Hoping to show some moral support, Bree reached across the counter and patted her arm. "I know I can trust you not to say anything about this to anyone. Derek's aware that I'm a reporter, and he won't talk to me candidly. You can steer the conversation around to money, ask about investments in the area, something like that. He might offer up information he shouldn't, just to impress you. It's worth a shot."

"This is a very small town, and while I'm no crusader, I've never hidden my views from anyone. He probably knows I'm against the development."

That hadn't occurred to Bree, but she sensed Julia was teetering on the verge of agreeing to help. This was important, and she wasn't about to let anything derail her plan. "You can tell him you're interested in more details about the project. That wouldn't be lying, and it will give him a chance to brag a little."

That got her a flicker of a smile. "Appeal to his male ego, you mean."

"Exactly. If I'm wrong about his involvement, only you and I will know about it, and there's no harm done."

"What if you're right?" Julia asked, her brow puckering with concern. "Derek's more or less the mayor already. No one's running against him."

Bree relayed Mavis's prediction, and Julia's frown deepened. "Cooper doesn't want the job. He never did."

"But if Derek really is cozied up with this developer, Cooper would run, to make sure the town has a choice."

"I suppose." Julia picked at the shipping label, obviously trying to buy herself some time.

Patience wasn't Bree's strong point, but she quietly waited for Julia to make up her mind. She knew she was asking a lot of her new friend, but it was the only way to force Derek to reveal his true intentions before the unsuspecting residents of Holiday Harbor handed over control of their town's future to him.

How she'd explain it to Cooper was another problem entirely. She'd think about that later.

"If I agree to this, it has to be legal," Julia said in a firm voice. "I won't record him without his knowledge, or search his office or anything like that."

Bree nodded in understanding. "I'd never dream of asking you to. I'm not trying to put him in jail, just get some confirmation of the half conversation I heard the other night. What he's doing isn't a crime, but it's still wrong, and I can't stand by and let him get away with it."

"The election is only a month away, so we need to do this soon, I'd think."

"The sooner, the better," Bree confirmed. "Cooper needs time to let everyone know he's running."

"Do you think he'll tell them why?"

"I'm not sure." After the shock wore off, it wouldn't surprise her if he called out Derek for lying to the town—and to him. Like her, Cooper valued loyalty above everything else. Considering the stakes, trashing Derek would be totally understandable.

"All right, I'll do it." Sounding far from confident, Julia fixed worried eyes on Bree. "I just pray you know what you're doing."

"So do I."

"You do what?"

She'd been so engrossed in her conversation with Julia, Bree hadn't noticed the door opening. At the sound of Cooper's voice, Bree plastered on a smile and winked at Julia before turning to face him. "Hope the bakery gets a cappuccino machine soon. I really miss my foamy morning coffee."

He didn't question her response. She felt a twinge of guilt about deceiving him, but she knew it was the best course for now.

Coming farther into the shop, he glanced around with an approving smile. "This is really starting to come together, Julia. When do you plan to open?"

"In the fall sometime, so people will know where Toyland is when it's time to do their Christmas shopping."

Cool and composed, she sounded completely normal. Bree knew Julia didn't feel any better about their arrangement than she did, and she smiled her appreciation.

"Sounds good," Cooper said. "Well, I better get to the office."

"I'll come with you." Bree tucked her pad back into her messenger bag. "I was just getting some input from Julia about business here in Holiday Harbor, and Nick's probably wondering where this week's installment is. Thanks again," she said to Julia, waving as they headed outside.

That was close, she mused as she followed Cooper next door. If she was going to keep her lead quiet until it was time to break this story open, she'd have to be more careful. Her mind was spinning so quickly, she barely registered anything beyond the fact that he had Sammy with him again today.

"He didn't like being left alone yesterday?" she asked as they entered the lobby.

"When I got home, he acted like I'd been gone a week. I felt really bad."

"You're such a softie."

He didn't say anything more. When they reached his office, he motioned her inside and closed the door behind them. Feeling like a kid sent to the principal's office—and justly so—Bree fought the urge to start fidgeting. "Is something wrong?"

"That depends." Leaning back against his desk, he folded his arms and leveled a cool lawyer's stare at her. "What are you up to?"

"Local color for my articles." To prove it, she pulled out her notes and offered them to him. Anticipating just such an occasion, she hadn't written any of her suspicions down. "You can check if you want."

He didn't move a muscle, but his eyes still bored into her, unrelenting. She couldn't imagine how his former clients could successfully lie to him. They must have had ice water in their veins.

After what felt like forever, Cooper handed her notes back unread. "I'll trust you on this one," he said gravely. "Don't make me regret it."

Fortunately the phone rang and he turned away to answer it. Otherwise she would have had to respond somehow, and for the first time she could recall, she couldn't think of a single thing to say.

If there was one thing he'd learned near the end of his time with Felicia, it was how to recognize when a woman was keeping something from him. Now it was Bree, and Cooper was at a loss for how to handle the situation. He was glad she and Julia had gotten to be friends, for both their sakes. His mother had taught him long ago that certain subjects were "girls only," and he liked knowing these two had someone to share those things with.

He and Bree had grown considerably closer, and she'd opened up several times about the mistakes in her past and her dreams for the future. But there was still an unmistakable line separating them. The kind of line a man crossed at his peril.

While he considered several scenarios, his eyes drifted to the sofa between the windows that looked out on to the square.

What he saw there made him smile. With Sammy stretched out like a furry backrest behind her, Bree seemed perfectly content there, typing away on her latest story.

"Staring, counselor?" she asked without looking up.

"Admiring," he admitted with a chuckle. "You two look cozy over there."

"We are."

Sammy thumped his tail in agreement, and Cooper laughed. "I was also thinking."

"About?"

"I need the surveyor's map for the property one of my clients wants to sell."

"Okay."

"Not really. I asked Mrs. Andrews where it is, and she has no clue. That means it's floating around somewhere in Granddad's bizarre filing system." Pushing his chair away from his desk, he went to open the door connecting their offices. "If I'm not back in half an hour, send Sammy in."

"You're in and out of that room constantly. Why don't you just move your stuff in there and call it done?"

Feeling himself stiffen defensively, Cooper made a conscious effort to relax. Her suggestion made complete sense, and his mind recognized that. It was his heart that protested. "That's Granddad's office."

Her expression softened, and very gently she said, "It *was* your grandfather's office. Now it's an unused room next to yours storing things you need to have on hand. What would he think of that?"

Cooper wasn't crazy about how this conversation was going, but he recognized she was only trying to be helpful. "He'd think I was a nut, wearing out a perfectly good carpet."

She gave him a sympathetic smile. "I think it's really sweet how you've kept the cabin and this building pretty much the way he left them. But someday it might be better for you to change them, just a little, and make them yours."

He had to admit she had a point. Since he wasn't an eighty-year-old man, his taste ran nearly opposite to his grandfather's. But the man—and the places he'd inhabited—had been a constant in Cooper's life for as long as he could remember. "What you're saying makes sense, but I'm not ready to redecorate everything just yet."

"Fair enough. When you are, let me know and I'll help you take over that humongous space in there."

As he moved toward the connecting door, he nearly asked again what was bothering her. Then he thought better of it. She was a big girl, and when she was ready she'd tell him on her own.

When Cooper ran into Bree outside his office early the following morning, she gave him a quick once-over. "Casual Tuesday?"

He grinned back, and she gave him a suspicious look. "What did you do?"

"You'll see."

Mrs. Andrews was in Portland visiting her daughter, so he and Bree had the office to themselves. When he opened the door and let her in, she stopped in the lobby and sniffed.

"Coffee?" Cocking her head, she gave him an approving look. "You've been here awhile, haven't you?"

"Yeah." He handed her a cup with nothing but coffee in it and fixed his with a little sugar. "I had an idea last night, and I wanted to see how it would work."

"An idea for what?" she demanded, glancing around the lobby. "I don't see anything different."

"Come on. I'll show you."

Feeling like a kid about to test-drive his first bike without training wheels, Cooper led her back toward the private offices. From the hallway it appeared that nothing had changed, and she gave him a confused look. Grinning, he strolled past his own space and opened the door to the room that had been closed and dark for months.

This morning, light streamed through the two large windows, unimpeded by the heavy velvet drapes he'd hauled down and carefully folded for his mother to use in her parlor. He'd pulled up the antique Turkish rug, nearly choking on the dust cloud he kicked up while rolling it to be put in storage. Several framed awards and commendations he'd stacked in the hall would hang out front, a tribute to Granddad and the long, successful life he'd enjoyed to the hilt.

Bree crept in cautiously, as if she expected the judge to appear out of thin air and order her out of his domain. When that didn't happen, she turned to Cooper with a bewildered expression. "You changed it."

"I know. I figured it was time."

Still clearly confused, she shook her head. "Why?"

"It's for you. You said you never had an office, and I thought it'd be nicer for you to work someplace besides my couch."

Her mouth fell open in a rare display of speechlessness, and he laughed. "I take it that means you like it."

Gawking at him, she slowly nodded. "I just can't believe it. What possessed you to do all this work for me?"

I want you to stay, he nearly blurted before he caught himself and went with something less terrifying. Shrugging, he said, "We keep tripping over each other in my office, but most of my stuff is in there. This just made more sense."

"I know how big a deal this was for you. No one's ever gone to so much trouble to make me feel at home somewhere."

"Well, I figured it was time someone at least gave it a shot."

Finally he'd convinced her, and she bathed him in the warmest, most beautiful smile he'd ever seen. "Thank you, Cooper."

Eyes gleaming with delight, she wrapped her arms around his waist for a grateful hug. Returning that gesture was the easiest thing he'd ever done, and he wondered if it felt as right to her as it did to him.

Before he could second-guess his instincts, he leaned in for a kiss. As he felt her lips curve into a smile, he took it for approval.

Until she murmured, "We have an audience."

"Funny."

"I'm serious."

Groaning, he dropped his forehead onto her shoulder and angled his head to find his mother framed in the window.

"Morning, Mom."

"Cooper." Picking up her little pooch, she waved at the blushing reporter. "Bree. Lovely day, isn't it?"

Reminding himself that she meant well, he summoned a patient tone. "Did you need something?"

"Oh, no. Mitzy and I are just checking on our boy. You work so hard, we were worried about you."

Frowning, she rubbed noses with the little puffball, who probably couldn't care less about Cooper. But his mother's worry was genuine, he knew. Kooky as she was, no woman loved her child more than Amelia Landry. No matter what was going on, or where he might be, she remained a strong, steady part of his life.

Sometimes—like now—her way of showing that love made him crazy, but he gave her a grateful smile. "Thanks, but I'm doing fine."

"Bree must be helping a little," she commented with a coy look. "I mean, with gathering information and such."

Being a reasonably intelligent man, he wasn't touching that one. "I'll see you later. You and Mitzy enjoy your walk."

After hesitating a few moments, she set the Pomeranian down and continued on her way.

Once Bree and Cooper were alone, she finally gave in to her giggles and laughed out loud. "You're so busted! This'll be all over town by noon."

"I've got news for you—it already is. Folks paired us off the minute you decided to stay here instead of going back to Richmond."

"For work."

"More than a few of them think you stayed for me. Including my mother."

She snorted at that. "That's absurd. I never did anything for a man in my life."

"You really know how to build up a guy's ego, don't you?"

"You know what I meant. I'm here because this is where the story is." Before he could blink, her look turned flirtatious. "Although if someone asked me under oath, I'd have to say you're a pretty nice bonus."

"Thanks. You're okay, too."

"Now get outta my office," she ordered with a little shove. "We've both got work to do."

Bree still couldn't believe it.

Sprawled out on a leather sofa even more comfy than Cooper's, she surveyed the room that had been transformed by opening the windows and removing George Landry's heavy-handed decorating touches. She'd never liked working at a desk, but the mahogany behemoth across from her was an impressive sight. If she squinted, she could almost see the judge sitting there, scratching out notes on a legal pad.

Despite his resistance to changing anything related to the judge, Cooper had thrown open the doors of this hallowed space for her. Not only that, he'd opened his carefully guarded heart, allowing her a glimpse of something those models and actresses he'd dated in New York had never even gotten close to seeing.

Kind and compassionate, he was also strong and relentless when something was important to him. Instinctively she knew he'd be all those things and more for the woman he truly loved. The one who blinded him to the rest of the women on the planet and held him so close he'd never even think of wandering away.

Could that be her? she wondered, reluctant to embrace the notion. Because as much as she'd come to like Holiday Harbor, she wasn't sure about settling down here.

Yes, you are.

The whisper drifted through her mind so quickly she almost missed the message. She looked at the open connecting door, hoping to find Cooper standing there, messing with her.

Except he wasn't. She heard him on the phone, discussing potholes and how late in the year they could be repaired. Shaking her head to clear out the weirdness, she got up and searched the empty office, hunting for an explanation of the voice that wasn't a voice. A furnace duct that was feeding a muted conversation in from the lobby, a radio picking up stray sounds from another station, anything. Hands on her hips, she stood in the middle of the room, glowering at nothing in particular.

"That's not a good look." Hearing Cooper, she glared at him, and he held up his hands in surrender. "Whoa, really not good. What's wrong?"

"I heard something. Someone," she corrected, still irked by the experience.

"What did he say?"

"It wasn't a man. It was—" Waving her hands, she reached for something logical. "I don't know. It's hard to describe."

"You?" he teased. "At a loss for words?"

"Don't mess with me, Landry. I'm not in the mood."

Her temper had no effect on him whatsoever, and she regretted ever allowing him to see her softer side. He retrieved a file from the cabinet on the other side of the room, but he glanced back at her. "You sure you're okay? You look a little spooked."

"It was just my imagination, or someone walking past the window talking on a phone. I'm fine."

She added a quick smile to ease the worry in his eyes. But as he left her alone again, she glanced around her new office. It looked completely normal to her, but she knew what she'd heard.

And she wasn't fine at all.

* * *

Around eleven Cooper glanced up when someone tapped on his open door. Julia stood there, and he got to his feet the way his mother had taught him to do when a lady walked into a room. "Hello there. This is a nice surprise."

That got him a faint smile, and she looked through the connecting door. "Is Bree here?"

Julia seemed uncharacteristically nervous, and Cooper's trouble radar started pinging loud and clear. But she hadn't asked for him, so he tamped down his reaction and motioned to the neighboring office. "If you need me, let me know."

"Actually I need both of you."

When Bree appeared in the doorway, Julia visibly relaxed. They both sat in the chairs in front of Cooper's desk, and his vaguely bad feeling ratcheted into red-line territory.

Julia turned to Bree with a resigned expression. "You were right."

"Right about what?" he demanded. "What have you ladies been up to?"

"You won't like it." Even while she cautioned him, Bree fixed him with a look that went beyond sympathy. Clearly bracing herself, she went on. "Derek's been lying to you. All of you."

She relayed what she'd learned the night of the vote, confirmed several times along the way by Julia's conversation with Derek earlier that morning. The clever toy store owner had artfully led him into boasting about his lucrative involvement with Ellington Properties. He'd even offered her the same opportunity, which she wisely told him she'd consider and then get back to him.

Cooper listened in stunned silence, unable to accept that someone he'd known since preschool was capable of selling out the town to shore up his own precarious finances. "Derek's always had money problems. That's nothing new."

"This interest in developing Holiday Harbor *is* new," Bree argued. "I hate to say it, but getting in as a partner with no financial investment is brilliant. Wrong, but brilliant." Turning to Julia, she smiled. "I can't thank you enough for your help with this. I know it was hard to do, but you pulled it off beautifully."

Standing, Julia said, "Cooper, I'm so sorry. I know how awful it feels to discover someone you care about isn't who you thought they were."

"Not your fault, but thanks. Let me walk you out."

When he returned, he almost expected his office to be empty except for the snoozing Newfie. He was more than a little impressed to find Bree still there, curled up in the leather armchair, staring out the window. When she hesitantly met his gaze, he frowned.

His temper was simmering, and he waited a few beats to be sure his voice wouldn't come out in a shout. "You should've come to me first. This is some kind of misunderstanding, and it wasn't fair to drag Julia into the middle of it."

"Oh, come on! You heard what he said not even an hour ago. How can you think there's nothing going on?"

"Derek likes to impress people," Cooper reasoned. "Especially women. He exaggerates sometimes, but it's harmless. He grew up here, just like I did, and I know he wants only the best for Holiday Harbor."

"Not everyone agrees on 'the best.'" She punctuated her argument with annoying air quotes. "Derek's no different from the owners who want to sell and move away, but he's claiming he feels the opposite to trick everyone into voting him in as mayor. Then he'll set up another vote, convince a few people to switch their opinions and voilà—here come the construction crews."

She made it sound so plausible, Cooper wavered on the edge of buying her argument. But this was one of his oldest friends they were talking about, and he just couldn't make himself take that final step. "I've known Derek all my life, and we only met a few weeks ago. Why should I take your word over his?"

"Mine and Julia's." She rose from her seat, as if looking down at him gave her some kind of advantage in this particular debate. "I learned the hard way not to go to press until I have all my facts straight."

Frowning up at her, he shook his head. "You're wrong."

Rolling her eyes in frustration, she let out a muted scream. "No, counselor, you're wrong. I just hope you figure that out in time to save this place from the bulldozers."

With that she charged into the hallway, slamming the door behind her.

Chapter Eleven

Cooper spent the next few days stewing about his latest row with Bree. She refused to answer his calls, even though he saw her around town, from a distance, while she continued working. The office he'd set up for her remained as empty as it had been before, and he chided himself for being so foolish.

For all that, his biggest problem was the niggling feeling that it was possible—however remotely—that she'd stumbled on to something. He couldn't put it out of his mind, and the more he considered it, the more feasible it became. Derek's college loans were substantial, and he'd been complaining that opening his own practice was much more expensive than he'd anticipated.

Then, a couple of months ago, a flashy car entered the picture, along with the pricey membership at Deer Run. Even for someone with Derek's high tolerance for debt, those were significant purchases, and the money had to come from somewhere. His firm was no busier than Cooper's, which meant he had another source of cash.

Cooper ran through the list of usual ways for that to happen and came up empty. Unfortunately that left

Harry Ellington, with his deep pockets and big plans for Schooner Point. The trouble was he couldn't confront Derek without making it obvious Julia had shared a private conversation with him. In the end Julia's involvement was what convinced him that Bree was right.

She'd gone out of her way to enlist someone who could help her prove or disprove her suspicions. While it was professionally smart, Cooper understood she'd also done it to be sure she didn't falsely accuse his childhood friend of something this serious.

And that meant he owed her an apology. A big one.

Just before eight on Friday morning, Bree tapped on the antique glass door of Landry's Books. Amelia popped out from the back room, waving as she hurried through the store to let her in.

"Good morning!" she sang with a bright smile. "I've got coffee ready for you. Kona or French roast?"

Still foggy, Bree did her best to match the woman's enthusiasm. "I've never had Kona."

"We'll fix that right now. Come in and make yourself at home. We'll chat until the others get here."

Done in cheery pastels, three seating areas were arranged around a center island that stocked gourmet coffees and scrumptious-looking pastries. Wandering through the aisles, Bree saw everything from mugs to locally made jewelry to collectible stuffed animals.

For her, though, the main attraction was stacks of books, arranged on shelves and highlighted displays scattered through the shop. Flanking the door were floor-to-ceiling leaded glass windows that split the sunlight into rainbow prisms on the old wood planks.

Amelia reappeared with coffee and orange scones

that made Bree's mouth water from several yards away. "This place is gorgeous, Amelia. Like a cathedral for book lovers."

"Oh, this is nothing," she replied, waving off the compliment. "My treasures are upstairs. After you talk to the girls, I can take you up there, if you want."

If her collection was anything like Cooper's, Bree was in for a rare treat. Just thinking about him still made her mad, so she pushed the stray thought back and moved on. "That'd be awesome. Thank you."

"So," Amelia began, smoothing the skirt of her flowered dress. "You want to know what the women of Holiday Harbor think we should do for the future."

"I don't usually categorize opinions that way," Bree explained earnestly. "But I've spoken to the fishing crews and several male business owners to get their take. It occurred to me the women in town might have some different perspectives."

Sipping coffee from an exquisite china cup, Amelia's eyes drifted toward movement at the door. Standing, she patted Bree's shoulder in a motherly gesture. "I think you're about to find out."

As the members of Holiday Harbor's various book clubs filed through the door to join her, Bree stood and smiled. "Good morning, ladies. Thanks so much for coming."

"You want opinions," one of the bakery sisters told her with a grin, "we've got plenty. For one, I think development is the quickest way to ruin this place."

Several of the others piped up in agreement, and Bree smiled as she took out her trusty steno pad. "That's what I was counting on. Just so I have my facts right, are you Georgia or Carolina?"

"Georgia." The delightful woman giggled like a high schooler. "I keep my hair a few shades darker, but it doesn't help. Folks mix us up all the time, even though I'm a whole year younger. Ever since we were kids, we've both answered to either name. Isn't that a hoot?"

Not long ago a conversation like this would have driven Bree off her rocker. Now she found it charming. "Definitely. Thanks for the heads up on how to tell you apart," she added with a wink.

Another laugh. "Oh, that's a good joke. I'll have to remember that one."

As Georgia wandered over to join her sister, the bell hanging over the door jangled again. Bree glanced up to find Julia coming toward her. They hadn't spoken since the tense scene in Cooper's office earlier that week, and Bree wasn't at all sure where they stood.

Thankfully Julia ended that uncertainty by extending a graceful hand. "Good morning, Bree. It's so nice to see you again."

Swamped by relief, Bree smiled back. "Same here. I know it's early, so thanks for coming to help me out."

"Anything I can do, please let me know." Worry clouded her gorgeous eyes. "We all need to pitch in to save this wonderful place."

Her polite tone made it clear she didn't want anyone to hear about their caper, so Bree played along. Motioning for Julia to sit, she joined her on a wide love seat done in a floral print. "You've been all over the world with your parents. What makes Holiday Harbor so special?"

"The fact that I've been all over the world," she replied in a wistful tone. "Don't get me wrong, it was a remarkable way to live, and I've had experiences most people only dream of. But I never had a home."

She paused, and Bree gently nudged. "Then you came here."

She nodded. "A friend recommended it for a vacation. When I drove over the rise and saw the lighthouse, I knew I was home."

Julia's description so closely resembled Bree's first impression of the town's landmark, she felt her skin prickle. But she had to remain objective, so she dialed her reaction down several notches. "I know what you mean. It's a really special place."

"I'm so glad you see that. With your talent for writing, I hope you can convince everyone a big development is the worst possible thing we could imagine."

"You've read my work?" Bree asked, honestly surprised. "I had no idea."

"Your story about Sammy." Sighing, Julia rested a hand over her heart. "I just read it yesterday, and by the time I was done, I was in tears. You have a real gift for making people feel what you're feeling."

"Thank you."

"You're welcome. So, what would you like to know?"

As they chatted about the town and Julia's ideas for increasing tourism, the bells announced a new arrival. Focused on her notes, Bree caught a tall, familiar figure in the corner of her eye.

She knew perfectly well why he was here, but she smothered a grin and kept her eyes on what she was doing. "Did you need something, counselor?"

"A minute, if you've got one."

Taking the cue, Julia stood. "If you'll excuse me, I'm going to get one of those scones before they're all gone."

Cooper took her seat, but Bree remained silent. She didn't appreciate the way he'd treated her, and she was still peeved enough to enjoy making him squirm. The women clustered around the refreshment table made a good show of talking to each other, but it was obvious they were listening in.

Unfazed by the attention, Cooper looked her squarely in the eye.

"I'm an idiot, and I'm sorry."

She was astonished by how he got right down to it. No legal waffling, no excuses—he went straight to the manning-up stage, and she was impressed. Meeting his eyes, she saw what her revelation had done to him over the past few days. Shadowed from lack of sleep, they held a resigned misery that broke her heart.

Normally she held a grudge for a long time. Because this was Cooper, she forgave him on the spot.

Taking his hand, she gave him an encouraging smile. "We won't let him get away with this power grab, I promise. Look." Sliding her tablet from her bag, she woke the screen to show him the graphics she'd started working on last night. "I designed a campaign poster for you."

"'Landry for the Future,'" he read, smiling over at her. "I like it, especially the watermark of the lighthouse in the background."

"Much classier than Vote for Derek," she agreed, rolling her eyes.

"I haven't talked to you since Tuesday," he pointed out. "How'd you know I'd be running?"

"I knew once you came to your senses, you'd do the right thing." Resting her arms over the tablet, she leaned in with a more personal smile. "You're just that kinda guy."

That got her a wry grin. "Sometimes I wish I wasn't."

"I don't," she assured him quickly. "I like you just the way you are."

"I'm glad to hear that." Flashing her an admiring smile, he pushed off from the couch and got to his feet. "I really should get going. Could you email me that file so I can get it to the printer? Derek's been campaigning for months, and as a write-in, I've got some serious catching up to do."

"I've got their address right here. I can send it if you want."

He shook his head. "I'd rather it came from me."

"So no one connects me to this mess. Clever." Not to mention gallant. He was willing to take all the grief for his decision to run, rather than share the blowback with her. Amazing.

In typical Cooper fashion, he shrugged. "No need to make this worse than it has to be."

Bree pulled up the email she'd already drafted and sent it to him. "Done. If you need anything else, let me know."

"Actually I was wondering if you're busy this afternoon."

"Not a bit. Why?"

"Sammy got into something nasty yesterday, so he's gonna be at the groomer's most of the afternoon. I was hoping maybe you and I could hang out for a while."

The hopeful glimmer in his eyes was more than she could resist, and for the first time since shattering his bubble, she managed a genuine smile. "I think I could fit that in. Where did you want to go?"

He just grinned, and she laughed. "Will I like this surprise?"

"I think so. See you at one?"

"Sure. I'll meet you at your office."

He lingered a few moments, and she waited for him to say something else. Apparently he changed his mind and simply said goodbye before heading out the door.

"What was that all about?" Amelia asked as she strolled over with a friend.

Keenly aware that no one could know what had prompted Cooper's decision, Bree kept it vague. "Cooper decided to run for mayor after all, and he thought it might make a nice detail for my latest article."

"Run for mayor?" Amelia echoed, eyes wide with astonishment. "What on earth for?"

"You'd have to ask him that."

The observant woman studied her for what seemed like a very long time, and Bree endured the scrutiny as calmly as she could. Amelia obviously knew something was up, and while it was tempting to confide in her, it wasn't Bree's place to step into the middle of this. If Cooper wanted to include his mother in his plans, he would.

For her part Bree was going to do the smart thing and keep her mouth shut.

Chapter Twelve

Standing at the tip of Schooner Point, Bree left her camera strap looped around her neck and just stared. Situated about a mile up the coastline from the Captains' Chapel, the spot had once served as a lookout post, with rotating shifts of watchmen posted there to scan the horizon for incoming ships, Cooper explained. Their job was to identify them as quickly as possible, so the town would know who was coming—and if they were friendly or not.

Soaring a hundred feet above the sea, the highest ground in Holiday Harbor felt like an island, completely isolated from the surrounding grassland and trees. Its unique shape mimicked the lines of an old schooner, which had inspired the name.

"This is incredible," she said with admiration.

"I thought you might like seeing what all the fuss is about."

"If I was going to build a bunch of houses around a golf course, this is where I'd put them, too."

"You're not helping," Cooper scolded, unrolling the proposed site plans across the hood of his Jeep.

Hoping to avoid a lot of questions, he'd intentionally parked in the shelter of a stand of oaks where no one could see him. Bree appeared near his shoulder and peered in at what he was doing. "What's this?"

"There's fourteen residential properties on here. And at least ten owners of vacant land stretching across the bluff."

Cooper tapped the incomplete list of landowners Granddad had filed under *T* in a file marked Traitors. Cooper had had to go through every drawer in the old cabinets, but when he finally found it, he grinned at the old man's opinion. "There's a bunch of folks in the Sell column, along with some of the people who've been calling me."

"Oh, no," she groaned. "That doesn't sound good. How many calls did you get?"

"Enough that I quit counting."

"I see five who definitely want to sell. What about the others?"

Cooper shrugged. "Some want to stay, some said if the price is right they might sell this property and buy another one nearby. A bunch of them insisted they'd pull up stakes rather than be neighbors to a snobby development full of mansions and fancy foreign cars."

"That last one was Jack, wasn't it?" When Cooper nodded, she laughed. "Sounds like him. I love that guy."

"He's a character, all right."

"So," she commented, glancing around. "Is this part of the mayor's tour? Because I can tell you the ladies will definitely line up for a little one-on-one with you."

"They used to, when I was in New York," he confided with a frown. "It's not as much fun as it sounds."

She sighed. "Yeah, I know what you mean. Sometimes it's hard to find that special person."

The revelation surprised him, since the cagey reporter had gone out of her way to keep that kind of personal detail to herself. Cooper took it as a sign that she viewed him as something other than a source of information. "You will. You just have to keep an open mind, so you'll recognize him when he comes along."

Her eyes locked with his, and a jumble of emotions passed through them. Hesitation first, then wariness. The one that settled in was wistful, as if she'd found what she wanted but didn't know how to ask for it.

Cooper wasn't one for taking risks, but this one seemed worth it. Moving slowly, he eased closer, giving her time to pull away. When she didn't, he leaned in and gently kissed her. Drawing back, he gazed into those dark eyes for some clue about what she was feeling.

Reaching up, she rested her hand on his cheek and pulled him in for another, longer kiss. He gathered her into his arms, amazed at the way she fit against him, filling all the empty spaces he'd tried so hard to ignore.

This time Bree broke away with a troubled look. "I'm leaving at the end of the summer."

He was tempted to argue that as a freelance reporter, she wasn't bound to anything with her job, and she was welcome to stay as long as she wanted. It could be a month or a year—it was up to her.

But he feared her independent spirit would interpret that as pressure, so he took a mental step back and played lawyer. "Is that what you want?"

"Yes."

Despite the quick response, uncertainty clouded her features. He'd never been one to tell another person what they wanted, but he wasn't ready to give up on her just yet.

"Then we should make the most of the time we've got." Holding a hand out for her, he asked, "Would you like the rest of the tour?"

"You mean there's more?"

"If you like wild blackberries, then yes, there's more."

After another moment's hesitation, she took his hand and they headed for a nearby hedgerow. It wasn't exactly a promise to put aside her career plans and stay in Holiday Harbor with him. But it was a start.

Something had shifted between them, but Bree couldn't define it because she'd never experienced it before.

Strolling through a seaside meadow seemed like a very romance novel-ish kind of thing to do, totally unlike her. But while he relayed some more town history and pointed out various landmarks to her, she found herself enjoying this afternoon more than she'd have thought possible a few short weeks ago.

The fact that she was spending it with Cooper didn't escape her. It took very little effort to imagine more of them, filled with lighthearted banter and lively discussions about everything from music to books to politics. They wouldn't agree on much, she suspected, but they'd have a blast defending their opinions.

Discouraged by moving from one failed relationship to the next, Bree had always blamed the other person. It was easier that way, and required no soul searching on her part. Now she faced up to the qualities that had always been presented to her as flaws.

She *was* tough to manage, but attempting to keep her true nature under wraps hadn't worked very well for her. Instead she needed to surround herself with people who appreciated her drive and wouldn't try to tame it out of her.

People like Cooper, she thought with a smile. No matter what ended up happening between them, she'd always be grateful to him for accepting her just as she was.

As they walked, they dropped berries into her empty camera bag. Farther up the bluff, they found a large rock to sit on and enjoy their snack. The freshly painted Captains' Chapel stood out on its picturesque cliff, but beyond that she noticed something along the far coast she hadn't been able to see from the lighthouse.

"What's over there?" Bree asked.

She pointed across the harbor, and he answered, "A string of sea caves. Most of them are below water level all the time, but a few have upper ledges you can reach when the tide goes out."

"They look like the ideal spot to hide pirate booty," she commented, popping a berry into her mouth. "I wonder if anyone ever used them that way."

"I don't know about real pirates," he replied with a chuckle, "but when we were kids, they were a great place to *pretend* we were pirates."

"Was it really safe for you guys to play down there?"

"If you picked the right caves, you were fine. Some of 'em echo your voice back in a real spooky way, and we got a charge out of scaring people who were out clamming."

"Nice." Tilting her head in a chiding gesture, she said, "I didn't take you for a troublemaker."

Clearly unfazed, he gave her an innocent look that had probably rescued him from all kinds of scrapes over the years. "It was all Nick's idea."

"I'm sure. Although the scary-voice thing sounds like something he'd do even now."

"No doubt."

Cooper leaned back on his elbows, stretching out his long legs while the late summer breeze rustled through his sun-streaked hair. He made quite the picture, but she decided to follow his advice to forego the camera and just enjoy the view. The relaxed, confident pose captured the essence of who he was, and she drank in the image, trying to cement it in her memory.

She'd never gone mushy over anyone in her life, and the knowledge that she was heading in that direction was an uncomfortable stretch for her. Her parents' wreck of a marriage had convinced her that you had to choose: a successful career or a serious relationship. You might be able to enjoy each at some point in your life, but keep them balanced simultaneously? Impossible.

Sitting here with Cooper like this, the warmth of his kisses still fresh in her mind, made her think that maybe—just maybe—she'd been wrong.

Cooper and Bree were laughing when he pulled up in front of his mother's bookstore and parked behind Bree's car.

"Thanks for a fun afternoon," she said. "Normally I'm not a big fan of history lessons, but yours was very entertaining."

A rare twinkle lit her brown eyes, and he barely resisted the urge to drop in for another kiss. Reminding himself the center of town wasn't the place for private moments, instead he opened the driver door of the little hatchback for her. "Have a good evening."

"You, too."

After she'd driven away, Cooper turned to find Derek standing behind him. And he didn't look happy. "What's this?" he demanded, waving one of Cooper's new posters at him accusingly.

Cooper would have liked nothing more than to answer that question in excruciating detail, just to see the guy squirm. But he couldn't do that without dragging other people into the fray, so he shrugged. "Turns out I have some ideas for this place, and I want to see them get done."

"Just tell me what you have in mind. I'll take care of it."

Reasonable as his tone was, the desperation in his eyes gave him away. Until that moment Cooper had some lingering doubts about what was really going on, but this confirmed it for him. Derek was in this up to his neck, and the water was rising fast. If Cooper continued on as mayor, Ellington's plans were worth less than the paper they were printed on. And Derek knew it.

Cooper made a show of considering the offer, then shook his head. "Thanks, but I'd rather handle it myself. See ya later."

Clearly furious, Derek growled something incoherent and stormed off. As he got into his Jeep, in the rearview mirror Cooper saw Derek tear the poster to shreds and fling it into the air. Which brought Mom out from her shop, railing at him for littering her nice clean sidewalk.

Driving out to pick up Sammy, the last view Cooper

had was of Derek crawling around on his hands and knees, cleaning up the mess he'd made. It seemed fitting, somehow.

Chapter Thirteen

Before Cooper knew it, it was Labor Day.

Preoccupied with things other than tacking and trimming, he lost the boat race, and not on purpose, either. He took the good-natured ribbing in stride, and when Jack mentioned his pretty first mate being a distraction, Cooper didn't bother trying to defend himself. His male mind could only concentrate on so much at once, and these days he had a hard time focusing it on anything but Bree.

After their dustup over Derek, Cooper's frantic last-minute campaign had brought them closer together than ever. Now that she understood the full negative impact the development would have on Holiday Harbor, she'd become an unwavering opponent of the proposal she'd supported when she'd first arrived. And when the headstrong reporter opposed something, she made sure everyone within earshot knew it.

As they strolled hand in hand toward the square, Sammy aimed his nose toward one of the food tents and woofed his opinion.

"You're right, big guy," she commented with a laugh. "It does smell good."

"This is an even bigger turnout than usual," Cooper noted, keeping his tone optimistic. "We should get a solid vote for mayor."

"Setting up the polling for today was genius. Everyone's in town for the Labor Day festival, so you get them all together in one place, and everyone can watch Derek go down."

He chuckled. "You're so sure I'll win?"

"Absolutely."

Her belief in him made him feel a little more confident than he had earlier, and he gave her hand a grateful squeeze. "Thanks."

"Any predictions on how it'll turn out?"

Skimming the festive gathering, he shrugged. "With these folks, you never can tell. I was up most of the night wondering."

"You mean worrying," she corrected him with a frown.

Cooper was aware he could do nothing more to influence the outcome of the election, and he refused to spoil such a beautiful day with negativity. Putting it out of his mind, he said, "I think Sammy earned himself a bratwurst during that race. Would you like something?"

"Evading the question, counselor?" Amusement twinkling in her eyes, she arched an accusing brow. "That's not like you."

"I'd just rather not talk about it till we know the results."

"Fair enough. I'll have one of whatever smells best." She took the corner of a partially empty bench, and the Newfie dutifully sat on the grass beside her. "We'll save you a seat."

"Thanks." Ignoring the fact that they were in full view of anyone with a set of eyes, he smiled down at her. "Be right back."

Cooper threaded his way through the crowd as gracefully as possible, and was rewarded with VIP service at the bratwurst stand. Balancing three meals and bottles of water, he carefully made his way back to the bench. Bree was staring off into nothing, which told him her mind was churning away at something.

"Careful," he said quietly to avoid startling her. "It's hot."

She blinked up at him as if she'd forgotten he was even there, then thanked him with an absent smile. At first, her mental trips into the unknown had been unsettling, to say the least. Over the summer he'd gotten used to her doing it, and it didn't bother him anymore.

Sammy devoured his sausage with gusto, lapping at the water Cooper poured into a cup for him. Then he lay down with a contented sigh and closed his eyes.

In between bites, Cooper chuckled. "Wish I could just chill out like that."

Bree didn't answer, and he glanced over to find her gazing at the lighthouse, a wistful expression on her face.

"I'm really going to miss this place," she murmured. "When I first got here, I couldn't wait to leave, and now it's the last thing I want to do."

Hearing that boosted his heart into his throat, and it was all he could do not to jump up and promise her anything she wanted if she'd only agree to stay. Leaning back, he casually stretched his arm out behind her on top of the bench. "Well, you could hang around a while longer, dig up a few more stories around the area. You've got an office now and everything."

When her eyes met his, he saw all manner of conflicting emotions swirling around in them. His gut told him she wanted the same thing he did, but she was afraid to admit it. Slowly, she shook her head. "I can't."

He gave her a smile of encouragement. If she did decide to stay, it would mean that change of heart he'd sensed not long ago was taking hold, significantly altering the way she'd live her life from now on. It was a big step, and he wanted her to know she wouldn't be taking it alone. "Sure you can."

"I shouldn't."

That was different, and being a writer, she knew it. The first indicated an inability to do something. The second was a choice. Her choice, because he'd never try to coerce her into doing anything she didn't feel right about.

Even if that meant letting her walk away from him. "Okay. I get it."

"I'm sorry, Cooper. I feel awful."

The comment passed so quickly, he almost missed it. But her simple confession held a deeper meaning, and he twisted to face her as hope bubbled up inside him. "What did you say?"

"That I feel awful. You've been so great, and I— what?"

This wasn't the place to discuss something so personal, but he didn't want to let the moment escape him while he whisked her away to somewhere more private. He moved closer, leaning in to avoid being overheard.

"You said 'I feel,'" he explained patiently. "Not I see,

or I think, but I feel. You've been here for two months, and I've never heard you say that."

Something akin to panic filled her eyes, and she glowered at him like a child caught misbehaving. "They're just words."

"I don't believe that, and neither do you. Feeling is different from thinking, and you're starting to figure that out. That's why you don't want to leave, even though it makes sense for you to go. Because like it or not, all this—" he swept a hand through the air "—means something to you."

"It wasn't supposed to," she confided in a strained whisper. "I was supposed to come here, do my job and move on." Hanging her head, she stared down at her hands in a dejected pose that nearly broke his heart.

Tipping her chin up, he looked into her eyes and smiled. "Life doesn't always work out the way we planned. Sometimes the things that happen to us instead are even better."

He added a gentle kiss, and felt her lips trembling under his. When he drew back, tears were welling in her eyes.

"You're making this harder," she accused in a watery voice.

"Yeah, I am, because I don't want you to go."

"Why?"

This was his big chance. If he told her the truth, he suspected she wouldn't take it well. But if he let her leave without telling her, he'd never be able to live with himself.

So he took a deep breath and jumped. "Because I love you."

It took a few seconds to sink in, and then she blinked at him like a startled owl. "No, you don't."

Not the response he'd have preferred, but it was Bree to the core, and he couldn't keep back a grin. "Yeah, I do."

"I can't imagine why," she scoffed. "All we do is fight."

"Debate. As a lawyer, I appreciate you going to so much trouble to help me keep my skills sharp. Never know when I might need 'em."

She hadn't said she loved him, he noted. But she hadn't said she didn't, either. He wasn't sure what to make of that, and judging by her perplexed frown, neither was she.

"No guy's ever said he loved me," she confessed in a bewildered tone. "At least, not one who meant it."

"You know I do."

Clearly still rattled, she nodded, but he felt her edging away from him. "I have to go."

She stood, and he followed, careful to allow her plenty of space. Hoping he sounded casual, he asked, "Was it something I said?"

"No. Yes," she amended quickly, shaking her head as she backpedaled away from him. "I don't know."

Cooper longed to reel her in for a hug, to hold her in his arms one more time before she fled. But she didn't give him the chance.

As she hurried away from him, Sammy whined his opinion of the whole scene. Looking down at the Newfie, Cooper sighed. "Kinda blew that one, didn't I?"

"I'm headed out to the Andrews place for our bridge game," Mavis announced as she pulled on a slightly less tattered sweater than the one she wore every day. "Are you sure you'll be okay here alone?"

"Don't worry about me." From her perch in the parlor window seat, Bree lifted her steno pad and waved it as proof. "I've got more than enough to keep me busy."

Good thing, too, she added silently. She needed something to keep her mind off Cooper and his stunning revelation. She still couldn't imagine what had possessed him to tell her he loved her. Especially now, the day before she was supposed to leave. Since it made absolutely no sense to her, she'd been trying to convince herself she'd misunderstood him.

The problem was, she hadn't quite managed it yet.

"All right," Mavis said, pulling her out of her brooding. "There's a storm coming in, so if the power goes out you'll find flashlights and candles in the hall cabinet."

"What about the big light?" Bree pointed at the ceiling. "What happens to that if there's a power failure?"

"It runs on a dedicated generator. When the town loses power, the harbor looks mighty dark, and any boats drifting too close to shore would break up on the rocks before they knew what hit 'em. But the house isn't wired to the generator, so you'll be on your own."

Being a city girl, she wasn't a big fan of roughing it, but she put on a brave face for her hostess's benefit. "I'm sure I'll be fine. Have fun."

"Fun, nothing," Mavis muttered on her way down the hall. "Tonight those two fancy pants are going down."

Knowing the nasty comment was nothing but hot air, Bree added the quote to her growing list of what she'd labeled "Mavis-isms." Inventive and very in-your-face, they formed a vivid image of the colorful keeper's widow she wasn't likely to forget anytime soon.

Her phone rang, and when she saw it was Cooper, she waited a moment before tapping the speaker feature. Calm and professional, she cautioned herself. "Hey there. Are you done counting votes already?"

"Yeah. Just thought you'd like the results while they're still warm."

His tone was friendly but not the least bit romantic. Having witnessed how adept he was at keeping his emotions under wraps, she couldn't assume anything from his current demeanor. Was he masking his feelings, or did he regret sharing them with her? She'd all but run away from him, after all. She wouldn't blame him for changing his mind.

Frustrated, she gave up and clicked her pen open. "Shoot."

"I kind of crushed him."

Typical Cooper, the understatement made her laugh. "Good for you. And for Holiday Harbor."

"I hope so. If you'll recall, half the town disagrees with me on the Ellington project."

"And the other half supports you. Once everything calms down, they'll all be back to their normal wacky selves and you can figure out where to go from here." Such a great guy, she lamented. What girl in her right mind would walk away from all that?

"You've seen a lot more of the country than I have," he continued. "Do you think more tourism will be enough to save us?"

She didn't, but for once she decided it was kinder to spare someone's feelings than be completely truthful. Maybe she was actually learning some diplomacy, and there was hope for her yet. "If anyone can make it work, it will be you, Cooper. You're the smartest, most determined man I've ever met."

She could almost hear him smirking over the phone. "Smarter than Nick?"

"Definitely." The humor blew away some of her tension, and she laughed. "Just don't tell him I said so. He signs my paychecks."

"Got it. There's still time for us to grab some dinner if you want."

Part of her longed to take him up on his sweet offer, spend one more evening with the most amazing man she'd ever met. The other, more practical Bree knew if she gave in to that temptation, it would only make leaving more difficult. For both of them. "Thanks, but I really need to finish this up so I can email it tomorrow before I head for Wisconsin."

She hadn't mentioned that to him yet, and she held her breath, waiting for his reaction. "So Nick found a new assignment for you."

Smooth and unconcerned, his tone was a dead giveaway. Over the summer she'd learned that the calmer he seemed, the more upset he was. "I'm sorry. I should have told you earlier, but I didn't want to spoil our last day together."

And then you said you love me, and everything went downhill from there.

"I appreciate that. What's the job?"

"There's a water rights battle going on in some northern towns out there, and he wants me to cover it."

She could almost hear Cooper frowning. "Sounds dangerous."

"I'll be fine."

"That kind of thing can get pretty complicated. You

talk to a hundred people and get a hundred different opinions. How do you feel about taking that on?"

"I'll be a journalist covering a breaking story," she reminded him, puzzled by the question. "I don't feel anything about it."

He responded with a sigh so deep, it sounded like he was carrying the weight of the world on his broad shoulders. "That, Bree," he said in a voice heavy with disappointment, "is your biggest problem."

The connection cut off abruptly, and she fought the impulse to call him back and give him a piece of her mind. Furious, she seethed for nearly a minute before deciding to leave things where they'd fallen. This was America, and he had a right to his opinion. She didn't have to like it. Besides, considering the childish way she'd behaved earlier, she probably deserved the scolding.

Mentally moving on, she scrolled down to the end of her story to pick up where she'd left off earlier. She tacked on the voting details and fiddled around with the conclusion until she was satisfied she couldn't write it any better. She reviewed it once more before sending it to Nick. When she got his confirmation, her job was officially done.

And so was her time in Holiday Harbor.

Leaning back in the window seat, she picked up her camera and began thumbing through the hundreds of pictures she'd taken. Most were for her stories, but a few were more personal, and she smiled at the now-familiar faces that populated her camera. When a shot of Cooper, Sammy and her came up on the screen, she paused. Clucking like the proud mother she was, Amelia had gotten a shot of the three of them on *Stargazer*.

Geared up for the Labor Day race, the three of them looked bright and happy in the sunlight.

Was that really this morning? After everything that had happened today, it seemed like a very long time ago. She wasn't a sentimental person, but she couldn't help touching Cooper's face on the little screen. As if his incredible looks weren't enough, he was also the kindest, most caring man she'd ever met.

And he loved her.

The truth of that settled cozily in her heart, even though she still didn't understand it. That thought led her to another, more vexing one.

Did she love him? In the park today she'd come perilously close to telling him she'd stay, to see where things between them might lead. Then the specter of her parents' torturous divorce had reared up to remind her just how awful things could get between two people who'd once loved each other. Bree knew it would be devastating to give Cooper everything she had only to lose him in a flood of bitterness. It was better never to have him in the first place.

A knock at the door dragged her out of her mood, and she got up to answer it. Outside stood Cooper, wearing the kind of yellow slicker she'd seen people wearing in no other place but here. "I'm sorry, sir, but I didn't order any fish sticks."

"Very funny." While rain dripped from the visor attached to his hood, he frowned. "I came to apologize."

Her foolish heart jumped into her throat, and it took a real effort to swallow it back down where it belonged. "Really? For what?"

"For being nasty and then hanging up on you. You're a frustrating woman, y'know that?"

"Hmm…" Pretending to think, she tapped her chin. "Let me see. How many times have I heard that?"

"You're not really gonna let me drown out here, are you?"

Grinning, she stood aside and let him in. "Just don't make a puddle anywhere. Mavis will kill me."

Slipping off his waterproof boots, Cooper hung his slicker on a hook over a rubber mat. "So, how's the end of your article coming?"

"Done. I just sent it to Nick, and he's beside himself. He said there was more excitement here this summer than in the whole time he lived here."

"He's not far off, I guess." Cooper flashed her a wry grin. "My next two years as mayor should be pretty eventful."

"Doesn't that bug you? I mean, you didn't want the job in the first place, when it was only temporary. Two years is a long time."

He shrugged. "Someone has to do it. Better me than some money-grubbing backstabber."

She'd seldom heard that kind of venom in his tone, but she understood it wasn't driven by anger. It was driven by love. For the home he treasured, and had come back to not because he'd had nowhere else to go, but because it was where he truly wanted to be.

In that moment something totally unexpected dawned on her. She'd fought against Derek, exposing his greed, because she loved the town, too.

"I finally understand why this place means so much to you. Why you came back, even though it's not always easy to live here." Heaving a resigned sigh, she added, "I get it now."

* * *

Her confession was so unlike the brash woman he'd gotten to know, it floored him. Maybe, with a gentle nudge, she'd actually change her mind about staying.

"I was thinking," he began noncommittally, "this storm is a doozy, and the roads will probably be a mess in the morning. You might want to hang out here a couple more days and leave later in the week."

"I can't. I reused my bus ticket, but my flight to Wisconsin is nonrefundable. If I'm not on it, Nick will have a fit."

So much for improvising, Cooper thought. "Well, then, the least I can do is drive you to the airport."

"That's sweet, but it's a long trip to Rockland."

"Not really. On the way you can read your article to me."

She tilted her head in that I'm-thinking pose he'd seen so often over the summer. "Are you trying to invent a way to spend more time with me?"

Busted. Normally he'd never admit it, but since she had him dead to rights, he figured there was no harm in being honest. "Yeah. I thought I was being pretty smooth, though."

"You were," she said with a grin. "I'm just good at reading between the lines."

No confession of love, he noted with a frown. If she was ever going to tell him, it would be now. That must mean she didn't share his feelings, and she was avoiding the subject to keep from hurting him.

He'd deal with his disappointment later. "Well, then, I'll go with you to the bus stop."

"That's really not necessary."

"I came to meet you when you got here," he insisted,

"and I'll walk you out. You're not gonna argue with the mayor, are you?"

Shaking her head, she rolled her eyes, but didn't flat out refuse to let him do it. It had taken him all summer, but he'd finally made some progress with the headstrong reporter.

He just wished she'd stick around long enough for him to enjoy it.

This time it was even harder to say goodbye to Mavis and Reggie.

Bree powered through their farewell without crying, but it was a close call. Her last view of the lighthouse and its keeper was the same as before: Mavis standing in the yard, watching them drive away. Sturdy and immovable, like the rocks surrounding the historic home she cared for so faithfully.

Tears threatened again, and in self-defense, Bree put a stop to the poetic train of thought. If she turned into a sap, Nick would probably fire her, and she'd be right back where she started before she'd begun working for him.

"You're pretty quiet this morning," Cooper noted as he drove with one hand and rested the other on her shoulder. "You okay?"

"Oh, I'm fine. I guess I'm just a little achy from the cold and rain last night." There was a persistent one in her chest that refused to let up, no matter how much she rubbed it. She must have pulled a muscle hauling her suitcase down the three flights of stairs from the tower room.

"You must have a lot more stories to tell your readers about your summer here. Real life adventures are the best."

The chipper tone in his voice struck her as being a little forced, and she turned to face him. "I want to thank you again for letting me do this series, Cooper. I don't know what I would've done if you hadn't taken a chance on me."

"You'd have figured something out." He added a confident grin. "You're smarter than you think."

Was she? Bree wondered. Did a smart woman turn her back on a strong, sensitive guy who told her he loved her, expecting nothing in return? The answer to that was obvious, but there was nothing she could do about it now. Her plans were set, and if she wanted a long-term contract with *Kaleidoscope,* she had to prove her recent success wasn't a fluke.

Thankfully her article was finished. As dejected as she was feeling this morning, she'd never have been able to give it the happy ending it deserved. Cooper stopped at his office long enough for her to say goodbye to Mrs. Andrews and Julia.

"Send me pictures when you open," Bree ordered while they hugged. "I want to see all those incredible toys."

"I will." With a trembling smile, Julia backed away and folded her arms. The tears welling in her eyes almost did Bree in, and she waved goodbye before they both started blubbering like babies.

Cooper insisted on carrying her bags, and after her overly emotional morning, she didn't have the heart to argue with him. While they walked, he gave her a sympathetic smile. "Nervous about Wisconsin?"

"I guess. I've never been there, so I'm not sure what to expect."

"You had the same situation here at first, and you did great. Once folks there get to know you, it'll go fine."

"I hope so."

The trouble was, over the summer she'd gradually come to grips with some of the character flaws that had caused her so much grief in her previous jobs. She had a different view of the world than other people did, and she now understood how that could make her difficult to deal with. Holiday Harbor was filled with eccentrics who cherished their own uniqueness and were generous enough to embrace it in her.

In the real world Bree feared she'd once again be written off as a wacky writer. She wasn't looking forward to the change. "So, what are your plans now that the town has decided to nix the development?"

"More tourists. Bookings are up thanks to your articles, but we'll have to figure out a way to make it work. Jack called last night with a plan for rehabbing that closed dock for sports fishermen and pleasure boats."

Bree smothered a grin. "Did he now?"

"He said he got the idea from you."

"I don't know what you're talking about. I'd never interfere in town business that way."

Chuckling, he went on. "Anyway, we agreed it's the best way to keep the vacation traffic from making life miserable for the commercial fishing crews. We just have to find the money to make it happen," he added with a wry grin.

"You will," she predicted confidently. "If you think another article or two would help, let me know. I've got plenty of notes I never used."

This grin had a hint of regret in it. "Thanks. I'll do that."

But they both knew he wouldn't. There was really nothing left to say, and they walked the rest of the way in silence. It didn't take long, and before she knew it, Ed was taking her bags and she had to say goodbye.

She started with Sammy, thinking it would be easier. His shaggy face hung in a canine frown, and he whimpered, standing on his hind legs to give her his version of a hug. Biting back a whimper of her own, she buried her face in his neck and tried really, really hard not to cry.

"You be a good boy," she whispered, ruffling his ears while tears snuck down her cheeks. "And take good care of Cooper, okay?"

He replied with a muted bark, tilting his head in a questioning pose. "I'm sorry, big guy. I have to go."

She glanced at Cooper, and got a faint shadow of his usual grin. "Is that apology for me, too?"

"I—" Her heart was firmly lodged in her throat, and she just shook her head.

"Thanks for coming to help us out," he said quietly.

There were so many things she wanted to say, but most of them would send her into tears, which would make him feel terrible. Instead she smiled, and he returned it with a halfhearted one of his own. He'd made it clear he loved her and didn't want her to leave, and she'd made it just as clear there was a job waiting for her and she had to go. But if he asked her one more time...

"I should get back," he finally said, leaning in to brush a kiss over her lips. "It was a real pleasure getting to know you, Sabrina Constance Farrell."

It took every ounce of restraint she had not to haul him in for a longer kiss. To savor one last time the inexplicable connection that had drawn them together from their very first meeting.

Pulling back, he smiled at her and made his way back down the sidewalk. As he went, she watched hopefully, waiting for him to turn around.

But he never did. And after a few more minutes she knew it was time to go.

She found a seat near the back and scrunched down, sliding on her headphones to block out everything but the movie on her tablet. Her mind stubbornly kept drifting back to Cooper, and she rewound to the previous scene three times before giving up. Switching over to music, she leaned her head back and closed her eyes.

Just as she was falling asleep, the coach lurched onto the side of the road, brakes squealing as it came to a stop. Curious about what had caused the delay, she glanced out in time to find a burgundy Jeep race past her window and disappear from view.

When Ed opened the door, a breathless Cooper flew up the steps and pointed right at her. "You. Outside."

She'd never appreciated the caveman routine, and it didn't thrill her now. But the desperation on Cooper's face silenced her sharp comeback, and she mutely followed him out of the bus.

"I hate to do this, son," Ed hollered, "but I'm on a tight schedule."

Cooper held up five fingers, and the good-natured driver chuckled. "Okay."

He thoughtfully closed the door, leaving Bree alone with a wild-eyed man she barely recognized.

"What on earth do you think you're doing?" she demanded. Now that her shock had worn off, she was more annoyed than anything.

In response, Cooper hauled her into his arms and

kissed her until she was breathless. When he released her, all she could do was blink up at him. "Oh!"

"I love you, Bree. I really don't want you to go."

The force of those emotions shone in his eyes, and she felt her own filling with tears. "No guy's ever come after me before."

"No guy's ever loved you the way I do, and you know it."

On the verge of crying, she managed a ragged sigh. "You're right. But there's something else you don't know."

Cocking his head, he gave her a curious look. "What's that?"

"I love you, too. I'm not sure when it happened, but I do." Smiling up at this wonderful man who'd risked life and limb to chase after her, she added, "But if I stay here, Nick's gonna kill me."

"Do you really want to do this story in Wisconsin?"

"Water rights?" She laughed. "Are you kidding? Snooze city."

"Then I'll square things with Nick, and you can stay." Leaning in, he kissed her more gently. "With me."

Bree couldn't believe what she was hearing. "Cooper Landry, is that a marriage proposal?"

"Yes, it is." He melted the last bit of her reservations with a warm kiss. Eyes twinkling in the sunlight, he smiled down at her. "Whattya say?"

Gazing up at the man who was generous enough to love her just the way she was, she smiled back. "I say yes."

Epilogue

"Now *this* is a honeymoon." Sighing, Bree stretched her arms out to soak in the Caribbean sunshine. "I love that there are places where it's summer in November."

Cooper trimmed the sails of their catamaran and dropped anchor before joining her on the long, padded bench. Leaning in for a quick kiss, he said, "When you told me you'd never been down here, I figured I needed to do something about that."

"I'm so glad you did." Happier than she'd ever been in her life, she smiled at her newly minted husband and draped her arms over his shoulders. "What did your mom have to say when you called her from the hotel earlier?"

"That it's been snowing since she left us at the airport, and they're supposed to get another foot by morning." When Bree laughed, he shook his head. "That's not very nice."

"Sorry. How's Sammy enjoying the snow?"

"She said he loves it, and he and Mitzy are getting along just fine. She was keeping him in the mudroom at night, but this morning she caught the two of them curled up asleep in front of the fireplace. She still has no idea how he got out."

"The Amazing Sammy." Bree laughed, waving her fingers melodramatically.

Grinning, Cooper kissed her again. "He managed to get us together, too. Not bad for a big pile of fur."

The love glowing in his eyes warmed Bree even more than the sun overhead, and she sighed. "It really is amazing here. How long can we stay?"

"As long as you want. Things are usually pretty slow around the holidays, and Granddad's old partner offered to take care of anything that can't wait. He can handle whatever comes up." Chuckling, he added, "I'm not sure Nick feels the same way about his ace reporter, though."

"I still can't believe he wouldn't come to the wedding," she complained. "I mean, who hates weddings?"

"It's not that, exactly," Cooper corrected her quietly.

"Then what?"

"It's complicated—and very personal," he added quickly when she opened her mouth to speak. "If you want more than that, you'll have to ask him."

"Well, in return for annoying the bride, he can make do without me for a while."

Cooper's expression made it clear he admired her more laid-back career plan. "If he fires you, you can always take Mom up on her offer to work at the bookstore."

"I'm doing that anyway, just for fun." Looking like someone who'd just seen Bigfoot, he fell onto the deck with a convincing thunk. "Oh, you're hilarious."

He clawed his way up the side of the bench and clung to the cushion like a rescued swimmer. "I must be hearing things. I thought my beautiful, very intense wife said she was planning on doing something for fun."

"I do lots of things like that now," she reminded him with a playful kiss. "I learned it from you."

* * * * *

Dear Reader,

I had a blast writing Bree and Cooper's story! They're so different, and they clash on pretty much everything, so there were lots of fireworks. Add to that a quirky little town on the edge of nowhere, and there was plenty to keep me occupied.

The sad part was they were both allowing bad things that had happened in the past to keep them from being happy now. Too often we take past results to heart and forget that the future is always in motion. Because of that we can change our story if we put our minds to it. Watching these two characters let go of their failures and move toward a successful future together was fun for me. I hope you enjoyed it, too.

If you'd like to stop by for a visit, you'll find me online at www.miaross.com, Facebook and Twitter. While you're there, send me a message in your favorite format. I'd love to hear from you!

Mia Ross

Questions for Discussion

1. The opening Bible verse comes from Corinthians: What is seen is temporary, but what is unseen is eternal. Being a pragmatic person, at first Bree doesn't understand it. By the end of the story, she believes it wholeheartedly. What does this phrase mean to you?

2. Cooper's life and legal career went awry when he was too practical and didn't listen to what his heart was telling him. Have you had situations like that in your own life? What did you do?

3. Cooper chides Bree for observing life rather than living it. Do you know anyone like that? If so, how would you encourage them to enjoy things around them more?

4. Mavis Freeman planned on taking in a shelter dog or cat but fell in love with a potbellied pig. If you've adopted a pet this way, what prompted your decision?

5. Bree remains completely objective about her assignment until she and Cooper find Sammy all alone at Sandy Cove. Something about the brave, loyal dog touches her, and she feels compelled to write a very moving article about him. Have you ever had an unexpected emotional response to an animal?

6. Because her parents' divorce was so painful for her family, Bree is convinced that her nomadic life

would doom a marriage and has never had a serious relationship. Do you know anyone who's put their career before their personal life? Are they happy that way?

7. Cooper revered his late grandfather. When he discovers that the judge decided on his own to reject the development project, Cooper is furious with him for behaving so unfairly. Has anyone you admire disappointed you in a similar way? How did you handle it?

8. Holiday Harbor enjoys some unique celebrations. Can you think of towns near you that hold similar festivals? Which one is your favorite?

9. The declining fishing industry is a real-life threat many areas face today. Is something similar going on near you? If so, what are residents doing to help solve the problem?

10. Cooper is content living in his tiny hometown, while Bree is a city girl. Which lifestyle do you prefer? Why?

11. At the end of the story Bree and Cooper are no more alike than they were at the beginning, but they agree that they make a great team. Do you believe that opposites attract, or are successful couples more alike than not?

REQUEST YOUR FREE BOOKS!

2 FREE INSPIRATIONAL NOVELS
PLUS 2
FREE
MYSTERY GIFTS

Love Inspired

YES! Please send me 2 FREE Love Inspired® novels and my 2 FREE mystery gifts (gifts are worth about $10). After receiving them, if I don't wish to receive any more books, I can return the shipping statement marked "cancel." If I don't cancel, I will receive 6 brand-new novels every month and be billed just $4.74 per book in the U.S. or $5.24 per book in Canada. That's a saving of at least 21% off the cover price. It's quite a bargain! Shipping and handling is just 50¢ per book in the U.S. and 75¢ per book in Canada.* I understand that accepting the 2 free books and gifts places me under no obligation to buy anything. I can always return a shipment and cancel at any time. Even if I never buy another book, the two free books and gifts are mine to keep forever.

105/305 IDN F47Y

Name _____ (PLEASE PRINT) _____

Address _____ Apt. # _____

City _____ State/Prov. _____ Zip/Postal Code _____

Signature (if under 18, a parent or guardian must sign)

Mail to the **Harlequin® Reader Service:**
IN U.S.A.: P.O. Box 1867, Buffalo, NY 14240-1867
IN CANADA: P.O. Box 609, Fort Erie, Ontario L2A 5X3

**Are you a subscriber to Love Inspired books
and want to receive the larger-print edition?
Call 1-800-873-8635 or visit www.ReaderService.com.**

* Terms and prices subject to change without notice. Prices do not include applicable taxes. Sales tax applicable in N.Y. Canadian residents will be charged applicable taxes. Offer not valid in Quebec. This offer is limited to one order per household. Not valid for current subscribers to Love Inspired books. All orders subject to credit approval. Credit or debit balances in a customer's account(s) may be offset by any other outstanding balance owed by or to the customer. Please allow 4 to 6 weeks for delivery. Offer available while quantities last.

Your Privacy—The Harlequin® Reader Service is committed to protecting your privacy. Our Privacy Policy is available online at www.ReaderService.com or upon request from the Harlequin Reader Service.

We make a portion of our mailing list available to reputable third parties that offer products we believe may interest you. If you prefer that we not exchange your name with third parties, or if you wish to clarify or modify your communication preferences, please visit us at www.ReaderService.com/consumerschoice or write to us at Harlequin Reader Service Preference Service, P.O. Box 9062, Buffalo, NY 14269. Include your complete name and address.

LI13R

SPECIAL EXCERPT FROM

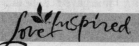

Gracie Wilson is about to become the most famous runaway bride in Bygones, Kansas. Can she find true happiness? Read on for a preview of
THE BOSS'S BRIDE *by Brenda Minton.*
Available September 2013.

Gracie Wilson stood in the center of a Sunday school classroom at the Bygones Community Church. Her friend Janie Lawson adjusted Gracie's veil and again wiped at tears.

"You look beautiful."

"Do I?" Gracie glanced in the full-length mirror that hung on the door of the supply cabinet and suppressed a shudder. The dress was hideous and she hadn't picked it.

"You look beautiful. And you look miserable. It's your wedding day—you should be smiling."

Gracie smiled but she knew it was a poor attempt at best.

"Gracie, what's wrong?"

"Nothing. I'm good." She leaned her cheek against Janie's hand on her shoulder. "Other than the fact that you've moved one hundred miles away and I never get to see you."

What else could she say? Everyone in Bygones, Kansas, thought she'd landed the catch of the century. Trent Morgan was handsome, charming and came from money. She should be thrilled to be marrying him. Six months ago she had been thrilled. But then she'd started to notice little signs. She should have put the wedding on hold the moment she noticed those signs. And when she knew for certain, she should have put a stop to the entire thing. But she hadn't.

LIEXP0813

"Do you care if I have a few minutes alone?"

"Of course not." Janie gave her another hug. "But not too long. Your dad is outside and when I came in to check on you the seats were filling up out there."

"I just need a minute to catch my breath."

Janie smiled back at her and then the door to the classroom closed. And for the first time in days, Gracie was alone. She looked around the room with the bright yellow walls and posters from Sunday school curriculum. She stopped at the poster of David and Goliath. Her favorite. She'd love to have that kind of faith, the kind that knocked down giants.

"You almost ready, Gracie?" her dad called through the door.

"Almost."

She opened the window, just to let in fresh air. She leaned out, breathing the hint of autumn, enjoying the breeze on her face. She looked across the grassy lawn and saw…

FREEDOM.

To see if Gracie finds her happily-ever-after, pick up
THE BOSS'S BRIDE
wherever Love Inspired books are sold.

Love Inspired®

A FATHER'S PROMISE
by
CAROLYNE AARSEN

When the child she gave up for adoption shows up in
town with her adoptive father, Renee must overcome
her guilt to find true love.

Hearts
= OF =
HARTLEY CREEK

Available September 2013
wherever Love Inspired books are sold.

www.LoveInspiredBooks.com

LI87836